HELD BY THE BRATVA

EVIE ROSE

Copyright © 2024 by Evie Rose

All rights reserved.

No part of this book may be reproduced in any form or by any electronic or mechanical means, including information storage and retrieval systems, without written permission from the author, except for the use of brief quotations in a book review.

This story is a work of fiction. Names, characters, places, and incidents are the product of the author's imagination or are used fictitiously. Any resemblance to actual events, locales, or persons, living or dead, is coincidental.

Cover: © 2024 by Evie Rose. Images under licence from Deposit Photos.

❦ Created with Vellum

1

CATERINA

It's two hours to go, and I'm already distracted.

I really should focus on studying. I have my final university exams in just over a week. But I keep thinking about the highlight of my days: seeing my neighbour.

If I leave at ten to six for my shift in the pub I work at, I see him in the foyer of our building. He's usually rifling through his post from the locker or chatting with the doorman. But he always looks up and sweeps his grey gaze over me as I walk down the last part of the corridor towards the front doors.

And I feel like I'm arriving at a ball each time, or like I'm a catwalk model. A beautiful swan, not a student about to graduate with a mediocre business studies degree and flap into the real world with all the grace of a penguin toppling off a rock. With him watching me, I could take on the universe.

He's way out of my league.

I don't even know his name. All I know about my neighbour is that he lives in the penthouse of my building—I rent the ground floor broom closet, sorry "budget accommodation"—and I want to have his babies.

My gorgeous, mysterious neighbour has silver eyes and black hair. He has a dark shadow on his jawline as though he shaves each morning but by the evening when I see him it has grown out to sandpaper.

And while at five-foot-nothing I could say this about many people, he's tall. He really is. My neighbour towers at least six inches over Steve the doorman who told me once he was five foot ten.

I didn't ask Steve about him, obviously, because I'm pretty sure I couldn't without blushing like mad. My crush on an older, serious, sharp suit-wearing man who probably has a wife or a bazillion girlfriends, is silly.

Tragic.

Especially given my non-existent love life.

I've never seen him smile. I seriously doubt it's possible. Would be a natural disaster on the scale of California wildfires and earthquakes if he did. The force needed to make his lips curve would be at least a seven on the Richter scale, and I'm pretty sure the heat from every woman in a five-mile radius spontaneously combusting from desire would cause damage.

Okay, maybe I'm exaggerating.

If he smiled, he'd only get women within sight pregnant on the spot. Maximum fertility blast zone of a quarter of a mile, I reckon.

I wouldn't mind being within range.

For the three years I've lived here while attending university, I've been daydreaming about getting my neighbour into my apartment and trying to tempt him to kiss me. As time has gone on, my imaginary excuses have become more detailed. I was thinking of a burst pipe, small cooking fire, dress that I can't zip up, or a massive sign saying, "I adore you, please take my V-card".

Because, yeah, after I get him into my lair, I'm assuming he'd guide me. He has that quietly-in-charge vibe. In my daydreams, he's overcome with desire and then something-something-something, fuzzy nakedness, him filling the aching void inside me, hair stroking, and good girl.

All based on daily interactions with a man who has never even returned my cautious sunny smile. I guess because I am officially the most socially inept person in London. I swear the only reason I'm employed at the bar is that I have a big smile and the music is too loud for anyone to notice my sub-par personality.

And here I am, musing about my hot neighbour who doesn't know I exist. I'm a scaredy-cat without a plan after my exams. I could continue working at the bar, but the whole point of "investing in myself" by doing my degree is to get a good job.

Ugh. I really should focus on... These black squiggles on my screen.

Maybe I'll just check my social media account—

A thudding from my front door jerks my head away from my distraction of a distraction.

I give a careworn sigh and get to my feet. This is not helping my exam prep. Honestly, how can it be that a girl cannot doom scroll and daydream while pretending to work in peace?

At the door, I peer through the peephole. "Hi!"

A man with a grave expression and wearing blue overalls is in the corridor.

"London Water," he says. "We need to access the pipes in your premises immediately. There's a bad leak."

"I haven't heard anything about this. Can I see some

ID?" My parents drilled into me about not opening the door to strangers.

"It's an emergency, miss. But of course." He flashes an insincere smile, like he's annoyed by my question, but raises a card to the peephole.

It clearly says London Water on it, though the name is almost totally illegible, maybe having been rubbed off.

"Steve isn't here?" I ask. The doorman is usually very diligent about escorting people in and out of the building.

"He said to come straight through."

Well. That's unlike Steve...

"Please could we enter before the leak gets any worse?" The man's voice is authoritative now, with an air of urgency. "Don't want it to damage your apartment, or for you to get into trouble for not being cooperative."

Shit, okay. Good point.

I hurry to unlock the door and the safety latch, and as I open the door, I'm tipped backwards by the man shouldering inside.

"Whoa! What—"

"Shut up, bitch." He grips my arm painfully and points a gun at my temple, and another man, this one in a suit, barges in after the first, closing the door carefully behind them. "Or you're dead."

2

CATERINA

Everything in me turns to ice.

Should I jerk away? He'll shoot me.

Should I scream?

Shit-shit-shit, I do not know what to do in this situation. Panic claws at my throat as overalls man drags me into the lounge and shoves me onto the couch.

"Don't fucking try anything," he snaps.

"Where's your mother's money?" the man in the suit asks. He has a gun as well, and the dark barrel is pointed at my chest. His eyes are brown, and his chin is pointy and recessed.

I can't die and I can't think. I'm a cube of ice.

"Where is it?"

All I can do is shake my head, because I have no idea what he's talking about. I jump as a glass crashes to the floor, and from the corner of my eye, I see the plumber man trashing my apartment.

"Your mother stole a lot of money from my boss," the man in the suit says, his tone as level as his arm pointing that gun at me. "And just because twenty-two years have gone by doesn't mean my boss doesn't want what he's owed."

"You've got the wrong person." But the co-incidence of twenty-two years being my age is sending me into a deeper freeze. My back is on the couch, and there's nowhere for me to go.

I'm going to die. I haven't even had a kiss. I haven't lost my V-card.

"Please, this is a mistake—"

"Caterina Hart."

I blanch. Whatever has happened, they know who I am. They are after me.

"We'll get that money back, one way or another. I suggest you talk. Now."

"I don't know anything," I protest miserably.

Some rapid-fire words are exchanged between the men in a language I don't speak. Italian, I think? Or could be Portuguese. I'm not sure. I learned French at school because when I said I was considering Italian as an option, my parents freaked out about needing to focus on subjects that would enhance my career.

I've never told either of them that I'd rather have babies and stay at home. I've worked hard for this degree now, and since the kids-thing would require a man, and I have the social skills of a small cabbage, I'll make do with a career.

The suit man pushes the barrel of his gun closer to me, and snaps, "Tell us where the money is, or this will go badly."

Ope. Put a star next to that. I'll make do with a career, *if I live*.

"Please," I say. Three years I've wasted, not talking to my neighbour. And now I'll probably never speak to him. "I haven't got any money."

I've frittered away my whole life. I just didn't realise it was going to be so short.

They say more, demanding to know where my parents are. Asking what the cash was spent on. What they did with it, where it is.

I say that I don't know. I repeat it because it's the truth.

I'm not fully in my body. I'm a bunny in headlights as the men get more and more angry. And all I can think is that I should have used one of those stupid excuses to get my neighbour alone. I should have just propositioned him, because now he'll never even know my name.

Presumably, my space-cadet thing makes the men believe I'm no threat. The taller one in the suit keeps his weapon aimed at me, but they don't tie me up or anything.

"Una stupida," the fake plumber says, and I don't need any language skills to translate that.

But in an instant, I can see that my fear of certain death has given me an advantage. The suit man's gun isn't directed right at me anymore, since he's looking over his shoulder at his companion.

They start discussing something in Italian. This is my chance. If I can just reach my phone, I can try to call for help. But of course, my summer dress has no pockets, and my phone is at my desk, out of reach.

Death because of lack of pockets is possibly the most feminist point ever made.

Crap.

Could I sneak over while they're distracted? I move slowly, my heart vibrating like a broken washing machine on a spin cycle. Keeping my gaze trained on the side of the man's head, I shift. They could shoot me, but for now... Another few inches. My muscles scream at the tension I'm putting them under as I almost hover on top of the sofa cushions and stretch out my arm. My desk is two feet away.

"Okay, I think... What?!"

At the words I turn, and the smack to my face comes out of nowhere.

I spin with the force of it, and unbalance, falling to the tiled floor, hard.

Pain cracks through my head and cheek, and for a moment it's so sharp it steals the air. The shock takes my capacity to move, to think, to anything, threatening darkness.

"Did you knock her out, you fuckwit?" one man snarls, and *yes. Yes, that's a good idea. I'm going to pretend to be knocked out.*

My hair shifts, and for a second I think someone is touching me. Then I realise it's blood.

Blood is seeping out of a wound on my scalp.

Rapid talk, and I don't know if it's because of the ringing in my ears that I can't hear, or just it's not English. Then there's the sound of cruel laughter, and steps. I fight the instinct to flee, because they're too close.

"We'll dispose of her afterwards. Work first," taller, black suit man says.

"Aw, you're..."

"You can have your fun soon."

I don't have to feign lying still then. The horror and shock numb me.

You dispose of a half-eaten sandwich you didn't want but felt bad about just eating crisps for lunch. You dispose of a receipt for a smutty book that you really couldn't afford but bought, anyway.

"But—"

"You can have your fun, don't worry," the black suit

man cuts the boilersuit man off. "But we need to search, since she's not awake to tell us anything."

"You look. I'll stay here in case she wakes up."

You don't dispose of a person with no idea what you're talking about and who the worst thing they've done is not recycle a glass bottle occasionally.

I don't want to be *disposed* of.

And whatever the man in the boilersuit thinks is fun, I am definitely not up for.

Listening motionless as they tear my little apartment up looking for something I don't think exists, a plan forms in my head. Outlines and fuzz at first, but then clearer.

I have to get away. If I can...

"Come and look at this," the boilersuit man says.

The other man hesitates, but I remain absolutely still apart from my deep, slow breathing. *Go,* I will him. *Look how unconscious I am. I'm not a threat. I'm just a silly girl.*

"What is it?" My guard's voice has moved.

"Proof."

"That's the mother, isn't it?" They sound like they're in the kitchen where I have a pile of post and a pinboard with recipes and some pictures of us all having dinner on my eighteenth birthday.

I have one chance.

I slowly lift my head. My hair sticks to the floor where the blood has congealed. But the lounge is empty. They're both in the kitchen, it seems, riffling through my possessions and chatting in Italian.

My arms are wobbly as I push myself into a seated position, then onto my feet. I move swiftly and quietly, my heart thudding loud into my ransacked bedroom.

I open the window silently, then wipe my bloody hair over the edge, as though I climbed out. Then I look around and toss out a hardback book I've been meaning to read. It lands with a thud.

"What was that?" comes a voice from the kitchen.

Breath held, I slip across the room, silently open the wardrobe door and step into the confusion of dresses. I pull the door almost closed—as it was when I found it—and slowly, so slowly push backwards, further into the wardrobe.

Rapid footsteps echo.

"Check on the girl—"

"Shit!"

I can't disappear into a different realm, but I can hide in the ridiculous space behind the pipes that run up the building. They create a tall, slim gap I've cursed so many times for being useless for anything except hiding a body. And right now, I could kiss the builder who installed these fitted wardrobes for his irritating laziness of putting those pipes there.

Because as I wedge myself into the cubby hole, there's a torrent of unknown words that are obviously rude, and my bedroom door bangs back.

"Where is she?"

I breathe shallow and slow, my heart vibrating.

"Get her."

I stare at the wall in the darkness and promise myself if they find me, this time I'll fight. No freezing up. I'll scratch and play dirty.

"She went out the window."

My stillness is probably some ideal meditative state. I don't think I could move without breaking.

More swearing. Italian. They're definitely Italian.

"That's a small window."

"She's tiny. Little girl climbed out. Look at the blood."

"I'll go after her. You finish the search here. If you find her, kill her. If she's on the run, she'll contact her parents soon, and we'll get her that way."

There's the pounding of heavy feet, but my ordeal is far from over. As noise from the bedroom and shadows spilling through the partially-open wardrobe door, show the man left behind is motivated. Guess he wasn't as convinced as his colleague.

I'm alone, and my only hope is being still and silent.

As he roughly drags things around, I try for a relaxed state of mind that will keep myself calm. A beach, right? Or mountains. A nice spa. But I don't think of those things. I think of my neighbour's approving but haughty gaze raking down me as I walk out of the building. I think of how, when I turn back as I walk away, he's always watching me, as though he's as addicted to seeing me as I am him.

There's the scrape of wood and a crash as the man overturns my bed, then curses when I'm not there.

Shit. No amount of silver-grey eyes or beaches contain the panic now. I press my lips together to keep in my hysterics. This is all so unreal. I'm just a dull, shy girl with brown hair who eats too few vegetables and has a mild Taylor Swift addiction, but now I'm a mafia target.

I clench my teeth as he searches the wardrobe. There's a clink as he shoves the hangers from one side to the other, and he kicks my pile of shoe boxes over.

But it's been ransacked already, and he's not paying full attention.

He steps away, and the next sound is him dragging out my chest of drawers.

And somehow, my god, I've never thought of myself as lucky until now... He hasn't seen me. This absurd space in my wardrobe has finally had a use.

I keep breathing evenly in the dark, as the man who will murder me if he finds me crashes through my apartment.

I don't know how long I cower in my wardrobe. I begin to shake after a while. My back aches from standing in the same position. My head throbs, and the blood dries on my forehead.

Listening intently, I try to make out what has happened. But it's not like the murder man left with a cheery, "Going now, thanks for everything!"

Tons of neighbours mean there are faint noises, constantly. I can't tell whether they're from upstairs, or the man is still creeping around.

Every time I think of moving, I get as far as shifting an inch, and then stop. Because what if they're just out there, in my apartment? What if they have surveillance? What if they're playing a long game and waiting for me to come out? There is a crack of light coming through the partly-open wardrobe, and it doesn't flicker.

And as I stand, stuck to the ground, I think again of all the things I haven't done.

My neighbour would have turned me down, for sure, but I should have risked it. I have one life, and if it's over, I've achieved nothing. Not like my mum, who raises money for her vulnerable children charity. Very successfully, and I've never thought anything of that until now. Not like Dad, who cared for me and built his mechanic firm from zero.

Most of all, I haven't been essential to anyone. No one has been overcome with lust because of me, or so in love they can't breathe. I've never been kissed and held and wanted. I haven't been pregnant and had the man responsible stroke my belly tenderly.

I'm a failure, and I'm alone.

And I guess, honestly, I'm a coward. I couldn't find the

courage to speak to my neighbour, and now I'm stuck in a wardrobe, afraid for my life.

When soft footsteps echo through my apartment, I'm too far gone. A tear trickles silently down my cheek, because I'm an idiot. I should have moved.

I definitely can't escape now.

Maybe I should have... What? Climbed out the window that my chubby bottom would have gotten stuck in? Or what if Steve was in on it and if I tried to go through the lobby, stopped me?

This feels like I'm a side character in my life. Just here to provide suspense.

The person, whoever they are, walks into every room, pausing at the threshold each time. But when they enter my bedroom—the final room on their brief tour—they don't stop. Confident steps come to the wardrobe and my heart takes off. A helicopter in my chest.

When the wardrobe door creaks wide, I screw my eyes shut and another tear emerges.

I can't cope. I can't do this. But I remain quiet.

"Moya koshechka." I don't understand the words, but the accent is different to the previous men, and it takes a few seconds to permeate my brain. "Open your eyes."

I do, surprise driving me. At the corner of my vision, a man has pushed to the back of the wardrobe and stands regarding me.

Shakily, I turn my head, and look into his titanium gaze.

My neighbour stares down at me, rage curling his lip.

"Who hurt you?"

3

BRODY

"Come here. I'm going to protect you," I add when she just blinks up at me with those dark-brown eyes I've been dreaming of.

She doesn't move, so I hold out my hand, gentle like she's a scared little cat. *Moya koshechka*, as I always call her in the privacy of my mind. My pussy cat.

Caterina reminds me of a sweet tabby. Straight chestnut hair that is usually in a swishy ponytail that begs to be wrapped around my fist. She's lithe and soft as a house cat. But she's wary.

"I'm Brody Marchenko. I'm your landlord. We need to get you to safety."

"But..."

"Now, before they come back." I make my voice deeper and firmer. I allow the inference that she mustn't be here, and yes, that's the case. But mainly because I don't want her to see me disembowel anyone who dared touch her.

"Okay," she whispers, and her arm creaks from lack of use as she takes my hand. I draw her out, but as she steps, her knees buckle and I catch her, sweeping her into my arms.

It's instinct, but oh god she feels so good, so right, tucked next to my heart. But this isn't the moment to relish that as I back out of the wardrobe and then stride from her apartment. In the hallway, two of my men are waiting. I give them rapid instructions in Russian to secure her home and the building. They nod and rush to obey, expressions serious.

They know that failure isn't a good option. I'm known as Dark Angel, and while I might not go in for ostentatious wealth and power displays like Westminster or Brent, I have silent, brutal strength and over a billion in assets that make me a dangerous person to cross.

"What...?" Caterina eyes my retreating men.

"It's okay." I carry her to the elevator, and once inside tell her, softly, "Press the button for the top floor."

"But you need a code for the penthouse."

"I have it." Given this is my building, and the penthouse is mine.

I say the code and she presses it in, hand shaky. Then the doors slide open to my personal space and a little of my tension unwinds as we enter.

Caterina is finally here, and she's safe.

"I can walk..." she murmurs, and I ignore her, holding her closer as I stride through the gorgeously-appointed rooms that she peeks at over my shoulder. In my en suite, I spot the comfortable but too-small armchair that the interior designer put in and I never fully understood the point of before now.

I set her down reluctantly and regard her, noting the drying blood and injuries.

"We need to get you cleaned up, and seen by a doctor."

"I don't need a doctor," she objects weakly.

I roll my eyes as I stand and go to the cupboards that contain all the essentials. This is not the first time someone who lives in this building is bleeding. Usually, it's me.

"Tell me what happened," I instruct her, and gather supplies as she haltingly tells me. With dressings and sutures and all the items needed, I kneel at her feet and listen while I clean her wounds.

The fucking Italians. As if they weren't dead enough before. They've been causing trouble for me for months. A pesky fly I've been swatting at half-heartedly.

But this. This is different.

Touching Caterina is *different*.

She's *mine*.

And any man who touched her is going to die.

I wash her cuts, taking care of each one and silently swearing revenge. I'd say it was paternal, since she's so much younger than me, but my feelings for Caterina are far from fatherly. She can call me Daddy, sure, but I want her with a savage, carnal edge.

"You're quite certain you didn't pass out?" I ask again. Her head injury has bled a lot.

"Believe me, I was awake for all of it. I'm not likely to forget," she says with a twist of irony, then hisses as I dab antiseptic onto her wound.

My fury that they marred my perfect girl is endless. The cut is in her hairline, and will be invisible once healed. But the bruise that's blooming on her cheek will be sore, and the monster inside me wants to rip the person responsible limb from limb.

She sits obediently and answers my all my mundane questions as I pretend not to know that her name is Caterina Hart and she's a university student. I know everything about her. I've been stalking her. Then I call the Angel mafia physician on speakerphone, and she answers all his questions, too. He suggests rest, and for her to be with someone in case she takes a turn for the worse, but otherwise gives her the all-clear.

"Do you think I should try to contact my parents?" she asks when I'm finishing the last of her dressings and she's holding an ice pack on her cheek. "They said my mother stole from them, but I find that hard to believe. She's so busy with her children's charities."

"When did you last speak with your parents?" The part about them finding out if she called them seems important.

"Last week they called and left a message. Dad said they were going on holiday, but that they'd be out of signal. They will phone me as soon as they can, and to not call, because it would cause problems. It was a bit weird to be honest, because they never go away. They're proper homebodies."

There's a lull as I unwrap another dressing and I think.

"Where did he say they were going?" I ask, a theory forming in my mind.

"He said... I didn't catch the name, actually."

"And did he tell you to do anything else? Other than not phone them."

"Only that I should focus on my studies and prepare for my exams..."

"And the call was from a blocked number?"

"Yes." There's a hint of concern in her voice now. "Do you think the same men who came for me got them?"

"Nyet. I think your parents have gone into hiding somewhere safe."

"Oh..." I almost see the facts line up in her brain. "That

makes sense. They didn't come to get me, but I suppose they couldn't."

If it were my daughter, I'd have faced any threat to have her with me. "Maybe they believed that by keeping contact to the absolute minimum and not telling you anything, they reduced the risk to you."

She smiles wanly.

I sit back and regard my work, checking for anything else I could tend to so she's more comfortable, while determinedly avoid looking at her luscious tits.

"Thank you for looking after me."

I give a curt nod because my throat has closed. My body obviously thinks words aren't necessary. But Caterina has no idea how much I would take care of her, given the chance. I'm too old for her. I'm a shadow, and this girl is sunshine. We can't fit.

"And coming to get me," she adds then pauses.

I don't know how to acknowledge this either, without it becoming a declaration of love and a possessive claiming. So, I don't. I busy myself tidying up the first-aid items.

"How did you know I was in the wardrobe?" she asks suddenly.

"Because I have one too. Bloody stupid, awkward little part of this building. I knew if you were hiding in your apartment, it would be there."

I don't tell her I was frantically hoping she had left for work early, and as soon as Steve was in the doctor's care and not actively dying, I went straight to find her. The bar owner hadn't seen her, and I raced back with my heart lodged in my oesophagus.

And that was when I found her.

"What do you keep in it?" she asks innocently.

Uh… Guns. Lots of guns. But I suspect that won't be a

reassuring answer right now. After her run-in with the Italian mafia, I don't think my being a Bratva kingpin will be to my advantage, and she mustn't go looking for trouble in my apartment. "Girls who ask too many questions."

"Oh!" Her face falls and I grit my teeth as though I could take it back by preventing myself from saying more.

"Joke." I wouldn't tie her up there. My bed would be preferable for us both. "It's okay. You can ask. I'll answer."

I'm pathetic for this girl. I adore her.

There's a beat of silence, then she asks, more tentatively, "How did you know I needed help?"

I glance over my shoulder this time. And this is easier ground, because although it was an instinct, a hunch, there was good rationale.

"Steve, the doorman. He was hurt by the men who came after you."

"Oh no!" Horror stretches her face. "Is he okay?"

I think of the blood on the floor of the doorman's little office when I went looking for him. "He's in the hospital. The doctor thinks he'll pull through."

"Poor Steve." Her brow pinches in apprehension. "I'm so sorry. I brought this to your door. Well, and your doorman. I should go. Not put you at risk from the mafia."

"That's not a concern." I can't keep the wry amusement from seeping through. Me. At risk from the Italian mafia.

Ha.

Bratva bosses are the most feared in London.

"But—"

"Nyet."

She blinks.

"If you leave this building, they'll see." She's not leaving my penthouse. I will protect this girl whether she likes it or not. "They'll know you tricked them. You'll be caught within hours."

She digests this eminently-reasonable argument silently, lips pouting and twisting from side to side as she thinks. And I hold my breath, waiting to see what she decides.

Three years. Three fucking years I have wanted her. I didn't believe she'd ever need me, and I was content to admire her from afar.

Until now.

I won't do anything she doesn't ask me for. There'll be no pushing, or coercion on my part. If this girl only needs someone to protect her, that'll be enough.

But I won't let her go.

She'll be my guest, or she'll be my prisoner.

She's under my protection. She's *mine*.

4

CATERINA

There's a long pause while I think of my apartment downstairs, and how much I don't want to return to it. I nearly died. I have to make the most of my life.

It's on the tip of my tongue to ask if I can stay here, or if Brody will find me another apartment in the building when he sighs, and asks, "Is that all your wounds tended to?"

"Yes." My voice has gone all high-pitched. My anxiety is out in full force despite my resolution.

I'm naturally shy—you don't make it to twenty-two never having even kissed anyone in a horny way without being painfully introverted—but until this moment I was more focused on my fear of what Brody had saved me from than who he was. Is.

He stands and I'm struck anew by how tall he is. How huge. My eye level is at... Yeah. It's at his crotch. My heart races. He's wearing a dark-grey suit that I suppose is wool, as it somehow is more sinister than absolute black. The fabric seems to gobble up all the surrounding light, at his command. Because although I can't see much more than his outline, that's easily enough for mine to respond. He's broad shouldered, and narrow hipped. And there's a bulge in his trousers that steals my breath.

He reaches down and takes my hands in his, and I look all the way up his body, unable to look away as he helps me to my feet. For a second, he keeps his hands on mine and my heart beats like a fluttering bird in a cage.

Dropping my hands, he turns abruptly and strides out of the bathroom, leaving me to scurry behind to a lounge with plush blue sofas. Gesturing at one, he sits in another. A safe distance, away, my brain fills in.

"Now." His expression is suggestive of an interview. Or an interrogation. "What would make you feel better?"

"I don't know." It's all over, isn't it? At least until I figure out what to do next.

But the emotions are hitting me like an aftershock. I'm worried about my parents—their holiday is too conveniently timed to be anything but their escape, but even so—I can't help wondering if I'll see them again. They might hide forever.

And my injuries are beginning to sting as my adrenaline reduces.

"What would you usually do if you were sad?" Brody asks.

Honestly? I'd probably obsess a bit over my hot neighbour. That was, after all, what I was doing when I was tense about my upcoming exam. I try to think of something more plausible.

"Phone my parents," I say in a small voice.

"Mm." His mouth sets in a hard flat line. "That's not a good idea."

"I know."

"What about ice cream?" Brody asks.

I nod, even as I'm confused. Yes, I like ice cream.

"Good," he replies seriously. This is an undertaking he's not taking lightly. His brow furrows with thought. "And revenge pizza?"

"What's revenge pizza?" He doesn't look like a pizza kind of man. More like a steak with a super-healthy salad bowl and protein-something with extra vitamins. Even hidden in the suit, it's clear my landlord is in amazing shape.

That he's my landlord makes him seem more forbidden, and my body likes that, sparkling at how naughty it is that he saved me and I'm now in his penthouse.

"Pizza with a thick layer of cheese, a deep crust, pineapple, and anything else that would greatly offend any Italian. Good *Russian* pizza."

I giggle, I can't help it.

"Something funny?" He quirks up one dark eyebrow.

"Good Russian pizza," I parrot back.

"Da. The best you've ever had. I guarantee it." And while he isn't smiling, I swear there's a twinkle in his eyes. "And a movie. Maybe *The Godfather*."

Trying to keep as straight a face as him, I fail. "What about a romcom?"

"I suggest you do not push your luck, moya koshechka."

He's so funny. Well, I think he's making a joke. He's also called me that a few times.

"What does it mean? Moya koshechka." I garble the pronunciation a bit. "It's Russian, right?"

There's a pause and his expression goes serious again. "Cat," he says eventually.

"Oh. Because of my name. And I guess you picked me up like a stray cat." I laugh awkwardly.

"You're not stray anymore." For a second I'm sure he's

going to say something else. But he only narrows his eyes and asks, "What movie?"

"One with a happy ending." I want the spark back in his eye. "Does *The Godfather* end happily?"

"Ah... Maybe torture by romcom will be necessary." And despite his teasing, he hands me the remote and tells me to rent whatever I like.

There's some devil on my shoulder that makes me scroll through while he's out of the room until I find an old-school romantic comedy that is as smutty and cringe as anything I've ever watched.

I'm so aware of his every shift as he sits next to me on the sofa, raising his eyebrows at my choice of movie but settling in and offering me a bowl of salt-and-sweet popcorn. Then half an hour into the movie, he rises and comes back with a pizza. I take in the ham, pineapple, and dripping cheese-covered pizza with a grin.

"See, savoury revenge with cheese is delicious," Brody says deadpan.

"Italians would be horrified with what you did to this poor, innocent pizza." I laugh, breathing in the heavenly scent of cheese and bread. It's good to make light of what happened today. I'm alive, after all. I'm eating pizza with my landlord, not sleeping with the fishes. I'm lucky.

"Exactly," he says with almost too much relish. "You'll want these, too."

He passes me a box of Ibuprofen, and I whisper "Thanks" as I push them out of the foil with a satisfying pop.

We stuff our faces with the most enjoyable pizza ever and sit side by side but not touching, watching the movie. It's oddly intimate.

I've only ever locked eyes with this man, and now he's next to me, passing me food like we're... friends?

Friends, but I'd like to have him inside of me. Friends, but I want his babies.

The movie is good enough, but not sufficient to block out my thoughts as my cuts begin to ache, despite the painkillers. But it's amazing how much better I feel. Like, I really could have died today, and when I expected it, all I thought about was the man next to me, who is now wincing at the bad acting on screen.

But still. I could be dead right now.

I grab the remote and mute the television before I can talk myself out of this incredibly stupid impulse.

"What do people think about when they're about to die?" I blurt out.

Brody turns to me, and blinks. "I don't know," he replies mildly. "What did you think about?"

There's a pause during which I regret all my decisions. Possibly including the whole surviving to begin this conversation.

"That I've never been kissed." *And about you. I was thinking about you, and how I wished I'd known you, and that you'd taken my V-card.*

"Never?"

I'm conflicted, because I'm revealing that I'm such an incredibly sad case that I've not managed to get a boy to kiss me in twenty-two years. I'm cringing. Blushing. But on the other hand, Brody's gaze just dipped to my lips. And it has stayed there.

And I'm supposed to be bold with this new lease of life. And he said he didn't want me to leave... So?

"Would you..." I guess I think he'll fill in the gap, to save me having to say the words. In my dreams he simply knows and kisses me without my having to request anything.

"Would I do what, Caterina?" There's a hard edge to his question, but I've had worse today.

I swallow and look into his steel eyes.

"Kiss me."

5

BRODY

She slaps her hand over her mouth in horror, as though the words slipped out without her permission.

"Sorry." Caterina groans with embarrassment. "I shouldn't have said that. It's just that nearly dying has me thinking of all the things I've never done."

"It's alright." I'm so impressed with how brave she's been today.

I should check if she means that she really wants this. I should ensure I understood her implication correctly, and that I'm not about to scare this sweet creature. But I don't, because that would mean I might not get to kiss her.

Instead, I reach across and cup her chin, feeling how small and fragile she is. I watch her eyes—like melted chocolate—as I lean in, crowding her. Stroking her face, I move my hand so my fingers comb through the hair at her nape and my thumb brushes her cheek.

"So pretty," I murmur. Then I hold her still as I tilt my head and lightly touch our lips together. It's as respectful a first kiss as anyone could wish for, but that's not what's in my mind as I withdraw just far enough for her to say something, but she doesn't, so I go in again. I think of my cock in her pink mouth. As I tease her lips with mine, I imagine tying her down and making her melt until she begs me to take her cherry.

I keep the kiss gentle but firm, opening her mouth, and when she makes a little mewing sound like the cat she is, sliding my tongue into the slippery heat of her. And I hold her in place with my hand as I tease and tempt her.

Every part of my kiss lures her to ask for more. I carefully craft it with seduction, even as I think of holding her down, pinning her hands, and thrusting myself into where she's soft and wet. Her mouth, yes, but more so her delicious, hidden little pink folds.

But despite the urges of my body, I just kiss her. Patient, gentle, but increasingly passionate. I'm determined to be what she needs. And it takes time, but eventually, she's trying things on me, too. Her tongue slips over mine and she explores my mouth. I catch her plush bottom lip between my teeth, and suck, and she moans. And then when I give her the space—I could win awards for how careful I'm being—she eagerly tries the same. I don't know whether to laugh or growl or groan. She's innocently sexy as she learns to kiss.

I guide her with the hand still in her hair to sit over my lap, and she nestles onto my thighs, though thankfully not pressing close enough to notice the erection straining against my trousers. Kissing isn't usually this arousing, but Caterina breaks every rule.

Because what starts off as sweet turns filthy. It's open-mouthed, bites and licks and dragging my lips over her jaw and down her neck as she arches and whimpers. At first, it's her tentatively resting her hands on my chest. But now she's pushing aside my suit jacket and grasping at my pectorals, and I'm glad for the hours at the gym because she seems to like my body. A lot. But not nearly as much as I adore her lithe young curves.

I've spent three years watching her go to work at the bar every evening, and knowing other men would look at her, and now I finally have her on me, kissing me back. The jealous and possessive monster in me is purring. I have her. She's mine.

Okay, she isn't aware of this fact yet, but details. Dark creatures of dangerous emotion don't care for technicalities. She's in my penthouse, on my lap, having eaten my food. I've got her now, and I'm not letting go.

She makes a squeak, but this one isn't the good, sexy type. It's pain.

"Caterina?" Simultaneously, my heart breaks that she's hurt, and I realise I've caused it. In the midst of my need for her, I forgot about her injuries.

"Sorry," she says as I release her. "I'm okay, it was just..."

A lump forms in my throat that she touches her face where a bruise is darkening her skin. She's still injured, and I'm awful for touching her in this situation.

"No more kissing where I might hurt you."

Her brow creases in disappointment. "But—"

"No, moya koshechka." The denial is painful, but I'm not putting her at risk of any harm. If I now have the right to care for and defend my girl, that also includes protection from me.

She presses her lips together.

"We missed the movie."

I think the movie has been over for a while. I didn't notice. Neither of us did. I grab the remote and rewind until she touches my hand to tell me to stop.

"It doesn't matter."

"It does. Watch the guy get the girl." She likes a happy ending, and she'll have it, even if I know she won't want that with me.

"I'd rather learn to kiss," she grouches, but obeys, huffing a sigh and crawling off my lap to flop into the cushions.

"We're not hurting your face."

And I mean it. I really do. I take a deep breath and will my erection down.

She's had a trauma today and needs to be treated delicately.

But because I am a bad, bad man, a thought occurs to me as I stare blankly at the television. Who said anything about kisses on her lips? I just assumed a kiss meant a mutual one, where she kissed me back. But that was a severe lack of imagination on my part.

"I could kiss you somewhere else..." That's as close as I'm comfortable suggesting, within the terms of my self-imposed rules.

Her gaze slides from the television to mine, and her cheeks heat. "Where were you thinking of?"

"Give me access to anywhere you don't mind me kissing," I suggest, patient as if I'm trying to coax out a shy creature.

Her stillness reveals she heard me, even though I didn't make the offer at more than a low rumble.

"Like, take off my clothes?" she whispers, embarrassment in her every curve.

I sit forward, gather the extra pillows and pile them behind her.

"As many or as few as you want."

Her eyes go wide as she looks down at her body, covered in the little top and shorts she's wearing. Then she visibly steels herself. Big breath in, chin tilted up, shoulders back. If that wasn't an inward pep talk, I don't know what is. I silently urge her on.

Yes. Yes, show yourself to me.

She sits up, crosses her arms, and I watch, unable to believe my luck, as she drags her top up, revealing that she isn't wearing a bra. She makes a squeak as the fabric tugs over her head, and I help her ease it clear of her dressings.

Then she has it all the way off, and I'm lightheaded at the sight of her exposed chest, smooth and creamy skin, little tits, the ideal handful. And her nipples, ohhh. Her nipples are pale berry-pink and round, and a bit puckered. My mouth waters.

"Fuck, so beautiful," I rasp out. "So perfect. Are you going to let me kiss your sweet breasts?"

She nods, and that's enough.

A sudden sound from the television makes her jolt, and she winces, touching her battered head. "Sorry," she says quickly, pressing her thighs together oh-so subtly, and a little smile tugs at her pretty mouth. It's so familiar from our daily interactions, and my affection increases for my shy, sunny girl.

"Don't worry." With a careful finger I guide her chin so she's looking over my shoulder. "Watch the movie and let me distract you. I'll make you feel good."

Lowering my head to her chest, I gently cup one of her breasts and place kisses on the soft flesh, avoiding the nipple as though I'm not aware that's where I'm headed. I keep it gentle, almost innocent, sliding my lips over to her other breast and paying equal attention there. The smallest hitches in her breathing tell me I'm going about this the right way. She relaxes as I glide down, covering her belly with kisses, until the urge to do more is irresistible, and I use my teeth, tugging oh-so carefully at her. Then love bites, sucking until she's covered with pale pink ovals.

My marks on her.

As gradually as I left her breasts, I return, but this time, I bring those rougher kisses too, and luxuriate in the way her nipples are peaked and ready. I lavish attention on her perfect young body. Yes, it's terrible that a man twice her age is the first to do this, but I'll do it *right*. Give her everything she needs. Her little nipple was made to be sucked into my mouth, and when I hold it between my teeth and lave the point with my tongue, I get a whimper from moya koshechka.

I redouble my efforts, heaping sweet torture onto her nipples and she heats, shifting and subtly but distinctively pushing into my grasp.

"Does that feel good?" I ask, knowing the answer and wanting her confession, anyway.

I can't help but take advantage of this innocent young woman. Yes, she might have dressings on her forehead, and a bruise rising on her cheekbone, but that only brings out my protective instincts in addition to my desire. She is more than the sum of her beautiful parts, and it's the person inside as well as the pretty packaging that compels me.

"Yes," she whispers.

Which is the perfect moment to ease back. She makes a sound of dissent as I slip onto the floor, nudging her knees to make space for my shoulders. Then as she cries out in protest, I catch her heel in my palm and scatter kisses up her calf. I languidly repeat with her other leg, and while I stop at her bare inner thighs, it's obvious she's turned on. She's needy, writhing her hips.

I look up and find her distracted from the movie, looking down at me.

"What about your shorts?" I suggest softly.

She licks her lips, and the space of time where I think she won't give me access to more of her perfect little body makes my stomach drop with leaden guilt. I'm a lot older than her. I'm the Dark Angel. I'm a wicked man, and she's an innocent. The fact I'm her landlord and she's a virgin college student gives my needs an even dirtier edge.

The contrast kills me as much as waiting for her response to my hint.

"Yes," she murmurs, and returns my life to me.

I sit back, giving her space. With tentative hands, she reaches for her shorts and undoes them. And I swear that almost undoes me, too. Lifting her hips, she pushes the jean shorts down and I can't hold in my groan as she reveals little white knickers. They have a frill of lace, and make her tanned skin seem even more golden, then she slips them off too.

So damned sweet.

"I'm going to worship every inch of you." I sound gravelly with desire.

I've wanted to do this for three long years. I'm not known for being patient, or good, but I've genuinely believed that Caterina was better off without me.

Now that illusion is shattered, I push her backwards onto the sofa. She's totally naked, and I'm fully dressed, and it adds to the eroticism and forbidden nature of this.

"Tell me what you want." I'm a monster for taking advantage of her when she's had a traumatic event and for forcing her to stay with me. But this is a line I won't cross. "Say it, in words, and I'll give it to you."

"I..." Her cheeks go scarlet, and she presses her lips together. "I can't."

That's a shattering, a rending across my heart. I draw

back, the disappointment making it ten times harder than a simple movement should be.

"No!" She grabs my lapel and I still. "No, please. That's not what I meant."

I don't move as she opens her mouth and shuts it again three times, attempting to speak as her cheeks get hotter and hotter.

"I meant, I don't have the right words," she whispers eventually. "I don't even..."

"Say it."

I think for a second she won't. But she visibly screws up her courage and says, "I want you to kiss me between the legs."

"Mmm hmm." I part her thighs and place a kiss on her mons, above the soaking wet, glistening slit where she needs me, then raise my head and meet her wide-eyed gaze. "Like that?"

Licking her lips, she makes a frustrated little sound. "Lower."

"Where exactly, moya koshechka?"

"On my... Girl bits?" Her face is scarlet, but she said it, and I'm proud of her.

Dipping my head to hide my smile, I lean into her pink sex, and put my mouth nearly over her clit, allowing her to feel my breath where she's wet for me. Such a good girl.

"Here?"

She whimpers and shifts closer. I press my lips to her folds in slow motion, open-mouthed and soft at first, then puckering to catch her clit just a little.

"Like that?" I ask, not able to tear myself fully away this time.

"More." She whispers it as though it's a secret she's keeping from herself and only telling me.

I do exactly as she asks. I take a long, greedy lick over her slit and she bucks and moans.

Tsking, I brace an arm over her hips.

"Watch the movie." I intend to make that impossible for her. "I'm going to kiss your soft little pink folds until you get your happily ever after."

This time I nibble kisses around her clit. I swallow down her juices, sweet and salty and heavenly. She's better than anything I've ever tasted. It's a delicate experiment as I try different movements, listening intently for what she likes best. But because of the television in the background, I mainly go by feel. Where she chases me, what makes her twitch, and when she loses her inhibitions and grinds her pussy into my face.

I gorge on her, and when she bucks, I follow, not stopping licking her. I'm addicted to the taste of this girl, and I end up holding her down to feast on her properly. Her cream coats my cheeks, and we're making an utter mess of the sofa. I couldn't care less. I devour her, relishing every bit of the evidence of her desire, from her movements to how soaked her pussy is.

Her hands are lost, trying to find the right place to be. Restlessly, she clenches her fingers in the cushions, drags them up her naked thighs, and tries to hover them over her belly.

Reaching up, I grab her wrist and bring it to my scalp. "Hold my hair. Show me where you need me."

"Oh my god! I can't..."

"You can." I give my voice the deep authority of when I'm issuing orders to my men, and that works, because not only does she slide her fingers into my hair and grip, she makes an involuntary mewl. I redouble my efforts on her clit, and when I feel her other hand on my head, and she screams and her pussy clenches under my ministrations, I smile in triumph.

It's long minutes of easing her through her orgasm. She's fucking beautiful as she comes. Wild, and uninhibited, pulsing and crying out as the pleasure sweeps her away and I gentle my kisses until I'm brushing my lips over her thighs.

Still haven't worshipped those padded beauties as they deserve, but I vow I will as I look up to find her with her eyes closed, then open and her gaze zigzagging over me and where I'm kissing her, and then glancing up at the television.

"Oh my god," she whispers.

Your Dark Angel, I correct her internally. *And your captor*.

But looking at her reminds me. She's had a long and emotional day, and while I'd love to see what else I can lure her into asking for, that's enough for now.

Obviously, I'd like to take that little cherry, but she's not going anywhere, so I can wait.

"Time for bed," I say, standing and offering her my hand. The television is quiet and black, the romcom having finished while neither of us were watching.

Panic overtakes her expression of beatific contentment.

"My apartment is ruined. I really don't want to go back there—"

"You're staying here," I cut in firmly.

"I can't do that. It's putting you at risk," she says miserably. "They're dangerous men."

"I think I can manage," I reply, and there's a cynical edge to my words. "And I can't let you put yourself in danger by leaving."

That skirts around the reality that I won't allow her to leave me, ever. But perhaps it's better if she thinks she's here of her own volition? That'll make her more likely to fall in love. I think.

Unless Stockholm syndrome is really quick? I should look that up.

I'm beginning to see the appeal of love potions.

So I lie. "Just tonight."

6

CATERINA

The happiest evening of my life followed on from the worst possible afternoon. I've been in my landlord's penthouse, having had my pussy licked. I'm practically drunk after coming on Brody's tongue.

He. Licked. Me.

And it was spectacular. The best happy ending to a movie ever.

Afterwards, despite a bulge in his trousers that looked as though he was smuggling a baseball bat, he didn't want me to touch him, and his expression remained as serious as ever. He just helped me dress, and then guided me through his penthouse.

The spare room is basically the size of my entire apartment, and luxuriously decorated in pale blue and grey and gold.

"What should I wear to bed?" I ask, a bit lost and still tingling from my orgasm.

"We'll sort your clothes tomorrow..." he begins, then scowls.

"It's okay," I say quickly, giving him a big smile, even

though I'm confused and the solution I'm about to suggest fills me with dread. "I'll go down and get something from my apartment—"

"No," he snaps. "Wait here." He strides out, and I instantly feel alone and a spare part, so I follow cautiously and look across the hallway into his bedroom. It's the mirror image of mine, in navy instead of this pretty, feminine washed-out sky colour. In a wardrobe are rows of hung shirts ranging from pristine white to grey to black like a shadow creeping across a bevy of swans.

Grabbing a white shirt, he turns and starts as he sees that I have disobeyed him, then approaches more slowly. Wordlessly, he hands it to me.

I suppress the urge to put it to my nose immediately.

"Goodnight." His gravelly voice sends a shudder of awareness down my spine.

"'Night." I want to reach up and kiss him. Perhaps ask if I can sleep in his bed. Beg him to take my V-card. And I nearly—so nearly—decide to.

But a lifetime of being a good girl doesn't get wiped away with one terrifying afternoon. So I don't. I smile hopefully, tilt my chin up and make myself available for kissing, and slump when he gently but firmly closes my bedroom door.

It's only when I go to the bathroom that I realise why, aside from my sparkling personality, he wouldn't have wanted to kiss me again. I look like a cross between an ogress and a mummy.

Oh god.

Brody is so kind. He kissed me and... My cheeks heat as I remember what else he did.

Agghghgg.

Probably it was all because he felt bad for the beaten-up

girl. What if he just feels responsible because he's my landlord, and I was in his building when I was... I don't even have words for what happened to me today. I guess "nearly killed" covers it.

Charity. Ugh, the very thought of him pitying me—trying to cheer up the zombie by giving her what she asked for—makes me cringe so hard I'm almost bent double.

I'm so embarrassed. If I could teleport to wherever my parents are hiding out, I would. I'd probably accept melting into the ground.

Thoughts swirl around my mind as I carefully shower and dry myself, then slip into Brody's shirt.

I give in and sniff the collar like an addict, and perhaps it's just my imagination, but I catch his scent. Seawater, neroli, steel, and musk. It's sharp and strong.

And that's when I realise what I have to do. Brody is way too kind-hearted to deny me, even if it must make him uncomfortable.

So. New resolution.

I am not asking Brody for things. I cannot risk it being just him humouring me.

It's probably a moot point, because I'll figure out somewhere else to stay—maybe try to find my parents—tomorrow. But anything that happens between us from now on will have to be because he initiates it.

In the morning, my resolution doesn't prevent my awareness of the man I'm sharing a space with. There are sounds of movement from the rest of the penthouse, and my squirrel brain thinks about Brody getting out of bed—I wonder if he sleeps naked?—having a shower, buttoning his collar over the sandpaper bump of his Adam's apple, and covering his body with one of those beautifully-fitted suits he wears.

I'm practically drooling at the image my mind fills in from the smallest sounds, but as I dress in my shorts and strappy top, I give myself a stern talking-to.

No lusting after my kind, extremely hot, and oh-so-serious landlord. No making suggestions. No telling him my deepest, filthiest desires. No playing the sympathy card.

As I see the curve of my breasts beneath my top, I add a new one. No attempting to catch his interest with my only-just-not-a-teenager body. He's twice my age. He wants a mature woman, probably a blonde who is as serious as he is, not a try-hard girl like me.

So despite having slept in it, and stayed up way too late with the awareness of my nipples pebbled on the fabric that usually lies against his chest, I slip his shirt on over my little top. It swamps me, but it covers me too. No risk of accidentally showing off my boobs.

When I find him, he's sitting in what seems like a breakfast room, sunlight spilling in from the windows, a newspaper spread at one elbow and a cup of coffee in the other.

I don't have to announce myself. He notices me immediately and sweeps his gaze over me from head to toe. Lingering on the shirt before settling on my face. I can't read his expression.

"Great bruise, isn't it? But you should have seen the other guy," I joke.

I look a fright. Even worse than yesterday. The bruising and swelling has developed overnight, and I guess it's not as bad as it could have been without Brody's care.

"I will," he mutters and adds more distinctly, "I had

Denis make you some breakfast options. I'm not sure what'll help your bruises though..."

"Cold revenge pizza?" I suggest with a smile, and he returns a wry look.

"That can be arranged. I have some business to attend to today, but Denis is at your service. No Italian will get past him, I guarantee. Now sit and eat."

I do as he says, and I don't know how I know, but that seems to please him. Not an actual smile, don't get me wrong. But something about the tilt of his head and the way his shoulders lower fractionally suggest he's more relaxed.

On the table is basically one of those breakfast buffets you see in adverts for expensive hotels. There are several silver domes, as well as pastries, toast, cereal, and jugs of fruit juice, tea, and coffee. Denis turns out to be a man in his sixties with a strong Russian accent and a countenance as serious as Brody's, but focused on what I'm eating rather than me. He pours me tea, that being my caffeine of choice at all times of day like a proper Brit, and under Brody's observation when Denis retires to the kitchen somewhat accepting that I don't eat much in the morning, I nibble on a strawberry.

"Thank you for this. I'll be out of your way soon," I offer.

Brody's brow furrows. "What do you mean?"

"Well, I need to..." I run out of words. Because I really don't know what to do next. This whole, "being a mafia target" doesn't come with a pdf user guide. Even if I was the sort of person to read manuals. "Either leave—"

"That's not a good idea," he snaps. "We discussed it yesterday."

I'm learning that Brody is abrupt and brutal in cutting

people off when he thinks they're making poor choices. But he's right.

"Get my apartment liveable, do my final exam, and figure out everything else after that."

"Don't go downstairs."

"I need to live somewhere." Homelessness is not fun. I've seen posts on social media, and I'll take my chances with my apartment rather than that. "Just until my exam, and then I'll try to find my parents. I think that's what they'd want." Obviously, I can't know what they want, except they were clear I shouldn't phone them.

"I'll find another apartment in this block for you," he says easily. "It might take a few days, though."

"Are you sure—"

"Absolutely," he cuts me off. "Your current residence isn't safe, and as your landlord, it's only right I provide you with somewhere secure. And you can stay here until it's ready."

"That's really kind." I toy with a strawberry and try not to wish that he'd offer for me to be his secretary or something. What he's offering is more than generous.

"Not at all," he replies, and I must imagine the twist of cynicism in his words. "Now. I have urgent work to do today—"

"Yes." I almost fall over myself standing up, even though I don't know where I'd go.

"And so do you—"

"I'll get out of your way." He's clearly a busy, important person, and I'm a bedraggled kitten he's saved. "I'm sorry for disrupting your morning."

"Enough apologising."

"Sorry."

He raises one eyebrow, and I smile sheepishly and bite

my lip to prevent myself from apologising for apologising. I just nod.

"I understand your exam is important, but I hope you could do me a favour before you settle into studying."

"Of course. Anything." Literally. If he asks, I'll happily do anything.

"Good girl." He reaches into his pocket and pulls out a credit card, which he slides across the table. "Use this, and purchase whatever you need."

It's matte silver, but shiny too, and gleams with wealth.

"I couldn't—"

"Caterina," he says seriously. "Your comfort is important to me, and I'm not having you return to your apartment for anything. And do not be tempted to send down Denis, either."

"That hadn't occurred to me," I say faintly. And truthfully. I've never had anyone to do things for me.

"Good." From underneath his newspaper, he nudges a shiny tablet towards me. "Use this. I've set things up for you."

"That's too much," I protest weakly.

"Underwear, dresses. That sort of thing." He doesn't seem to hear me at all.

I nod warily. I could do with some clean knickers.

"The other task I want you to do for me is care for your injuries. Ice every hour. Painkillers at four-hour intervals. Denis will be here all day and has instructions to provide anything you need."

"Thank you." I'm overwhelmed. Just when it seems everyone who cares about me has either overlooked or left me behind, I'm not dwelling on which, I have an unexpected saviour in the form of the man I've been lusting over for three years.

But this morning, he appears to have forgotten making me orgasm on his face, and me admitting to never having had a kiss. It's all about caring for me as though he's a hot authority figure, not the person I'd love to have babies with.

"No need to thank me." He stands and for a second he hesitates. He twitches like he wanted to lean forward and touch me. Kiss me, maybe. But instead, he straightens his cuffs.

Probably my bruises put him off.

"We'll discuss everything else when I return."

I spend the day studying and trying not to think about Brody constantly. I manage to access my university account, and I refuse to dwell on what happened yesterday, my parents, or what the whole thing means for my life.

I honestly get more work done than you'd expect. I look up a couple of exam questions, and do timed practices.

Admittedly, I go on a side quest reading about the London mafias, just to see if I can find out anything about my attackers. Each part of London is run by a mafia lord, but Angel, the area I live and work in, has a shadowy kingpin. The Dark Angel is more like a black hole: his presence is known more by the absence of where the kingpin of Angel should be. That and the way problems are mysteriously sorted in his territory.

The likelihood of any of the men who invaded my apartment yesterday being the Dark Angel is vanishingly small. The mafia who are after me and my parents are Italian, after all. Probably they aren't even a London mafia. So I spread my search wider, vaguely wondering what I would do if I discovered who was after me.

Nothing.

Currently, I haven't got any ideas for my continued survival better than begging Brody to allow me to stay in this apartment forever. The obvious problem is financial. If I can't do bar work, I can't pay my rent.

The shameful thought that immediately comes to mind makes my cheeks heat.

I could earn my rent on my back. On my knees. Pretzel-like positions? Absolutely fine by me with my hot landlord.

Thankfully, by the time I hear the door click and Brody strolls in, I'm focused on studying. Mainly. I'm curled onto the sofa in his lounge, the tablet he loaned me on my knees.

For a second it's exactly the same as when we meet in the atrium downstairs. I smile at him, and he regards me intently. The moment stretches out like honey dripping from a spoon, and as always, my tummy flutters. His grey eyes, so serious, and that jawline.

Last night I saw that expression looking up at me from *between my legs*. Charity or not, I'm going to treasure that memory until I am an old lady without a filter who boasts about having once had her pussy licked, and everyone rolls their eyes because they think I've lost my mind.

Given that for three years we've not exchanged a word, somehow, I'm not surprised that Brody isn't the type for chit-chat. Silently, he walks over to me, takes out his phone and after a second of flicking, passes it to me.

"Was this one of the men from yesterday?" he asks tersely.

On the screen is a photograph of a man with dark-brown hair and tanned skin. I examine the image. It's close-cropped, the man seems to be lying on a concrete floor, and his eyes are closed. I'm not skilled at racial identification, but I suppose he could easily be Italian. I try to envisage him in the suit, or the boilersuit.

"That's not him."

"Ah." Brody nods grimly. "Pity."

He takes the phone from me without further explanation or comment, then discards it.

My mind whirls. What was that about?

Standing to his full, intimidating height, he looks down on me, causing every thought that isn't pure thirst to fly from my head.

"Have you been a good girl and done all your studying?"

Oof. For him, I'd be the best girl.

"Very good." Do I sound embarrassingly over-eager? Yes, I do. "Actually, I've been more focused than I was yesterday. Even before... You know." Brody's apartment is perfectly comfortable, and whenever I wandered into the kitchen, I found Denis cooking and not happy until I took a sweet treat and hot beverage to my lair. I mean the lounge.

"And did you buy clothes, as I asked you to?"

"Yes." Sort of. I indicate the new shorts and T-shirt I'm wearing.

He glowers. "We agreed you'd buy dresses."

"Yes, but—" Did we? I missed that.

"I'm very displeased, Caterina." His voice goes deeper and hard.

That's an electric shock. Brody doesn't like my outfit? I don't know whether I'm indignant, or it's hot in here. Is it weird I'm glad I've got a reaction from him?

"I didn't realise there were conditions," I reply, treading right into "brat" behaviour. He paid for the clothes, so I guess he has a right to some say in what they are.

"How many things did you buy?"

"Only a few!"

"Show me," he snaps, and if anything, my response makes him appear even more cross than before.

I stand and for a split second he's so close, I can breathe in the scent of him. All the memories from last night rush back, and I long to be kissing him again. Then he steps away and tails me to my bedroom where I put the packages. It's a small pile, but I still glance nervously at him.

"You haven't opened them?"

I squirm, a bit awkward. "Not all."

He stares, taking in every part of me silently until I itch with embarrassment. I'm so clearly not up to scratch.

"Sorr—"

"Nyet." He sighs heavily. "This is my fault. I should have been clearer."

He scoops up the few packages with his big hands and I'm frankly confused as I follow him back into the lounge, where he shrugs out of his suit jacket and settles onto the couch I was sitting on. I watch as he roughly tugs off his tie and undoes the top button of his shirt. Then with slow deliberation, he flicks open his cuffs and rolls them up, revealing tanned, muscled forearms covered with dark hair, and strong, square wrists. When he finally drapes his arms over the back of the sofa, I'm practically panting. He exudes casual power and masculine elegance, I'm speechless. I've never seen so much of him, and every part is delicious.

He crooks his finger. "Come here."

7

BRODY

It's going to be more difficult than I expected to get Caterina to use my credit card to buy whatever she wants to make her happy.

Which is cute, don't get me wrong, but also very inconvenient. I thought there was a benefit to being a billionaire, but it's turning out to be more of a hindrance. If she's not impressed by being given a credit card you could purchase a small country with, how am I supposed to persuade her to fall in love with a morally grey Bratva boss twice her age, who she is going to realise eventually, has kidnapped her?

Back to Stockholm syndrome, I suppose.

She approaches warily.

"Show me what you bought, moya koshechka." I nod at the place next to me on the sofa, and she sits, careful that we don't touch sides, and my heart twists.

Not in love with me yet, huh?

She picks up a parcel and opens it with infinite care. Not ripping the packaging but sliding her little forefinger along the seam. My mind immediately goes to whether she'd be so gentle with my cock, and if I could tempt her to be impatient and grabbing and take exactly what she wants.

From the first paper bag she draws a relaxed sweater in a marl grey, and I nod. Not the cashmere I was hoping her to indulge in, but fine. Then comes a pair of jeans, and a plain top, not unlike the one she's wearing. From the second to last package falls a cascade of yellow fabric and my brows shoot up as she shakes it out and holds it up.

I blink, nonplussed. "What is it?"

She rolls her eyes at me. "A dress. Wasn't that what you wanted?"

"That's fashionable, I assume?" The material is silky, but the colour reminds me of one of those spring flowers in dainty floral arrays.

"Yes. No." She scrunches her nose. "Maybe?"

"Do you like it?" I ask, because honestly it's the only thing that matters.

"It'll look super cute on!" she assures me.

"Show me, then."

That stops her. Her gaze flicks up to my face to check if I'm serious. And yes, I am very serious about seeing Caterina in clothes she bought with my money. It might not be the signs of ownership I want her to have—a pregnant belly and a ring—but it's a start.

"Okay," she says shyly, and a wisp of dark hair falls over her cheek as she rises. My hands fist into the fabric of the sofa to prevent myself from tucking it back.

It's long minutes of tortuous waiting as she goes to her bedroom to change, and then she creeps back in, barefoot and although she peeks at me from behind a curtain of her hair, she might as well be a freight train. It's all I can do to keep breathing.

She's correct. The dress looks stunning on her. I wasn't

convinced by that pale yellow, or the cut, but that just shows why I know nothing.

"See?" She swishes the skirt to and fro. "Cute, right?"

I nod mutely. Cute is not the word I'd use. That dress is enough to incite me to rail her in it, literally anywhere. It's so sexy, for a man of forty-two it needs a health warning about the potential for causing a heart attack.

"There's one more package," I manage to say. Dying words. I'm well known for my murderous tendencies in the London Mafia Syndicate, but I'm nowhere near as lethal as Caterina in that dress.

She gives me an eyeful of her luscious small tits—totally by accident I think—as she bends over to pick up the last package. Standing before me, I subtly rearrange my erection so it's less visible as she opens the bag and peeks inside.

Then she quickly closes it again. "This is just…"

"What?" My curiosity is piqued.

"Nothing." Pink tinges her cheeks.

"Moya koshechka, there's no need to be embarrassed." It can't be any worse than me, a man old enough to be her father, getting hard from seeing her in a dress. Not even an especially revealing one. "Show me what you needed."

She whimpers with reluctance and pulls out a white lace bralette and a pair of matching knickers.

My mind fills in the image of her wearing them, and my cock throbs.

"I'll send them back," she stammers.

"Or buy more."

Her gaze flies to mine, her mouth an "o" of surprise.

"I don't need that." She twists her hands together. "I won't be here long. You said the other apartment would be ready soon. That's more than enough generosity."

"I was going to discuss that." My mind flicks through

reasons for her not to leave, considering the best way to play them.

This is like playing blackjack. Her apartment was a trump card, but now I need another, but I mustn't overdo it. Being a mafia boss in London for over a decade has taught me the importance of tactics.

"Law enforcement haven't got the men who came after you yet." As I say that, irritation rises in me that I haven't found the Italians responsible, and that Marco Brent, the only current London Mafia Syndicate member who is Italian, is being so bloody useless. The Blackstone kingpin has contacts though, and I'm hoping he'll come through.

"I didn't even think of the police!" she says in horror. "I should—"

"Don't worry. I ensured the relevant authorities were apprised of the situation," I say soothingly. The authority in Angel being me, that wasn't very difficult. "There's nothing you need to do except stay safe until the men are caught."

"They're mafia though…" She worries her bottom lip with her teeth. "I don't want them coming after you."

"That's not a concern for me." And I can't help the patronising tone that sneaks into my words. But since I'm keeping from her that I'm the kingpin of Angel for now, her safety isn't the best reason for her to stay with me. "But your welfare is. This must be playing on your mind, and you mentioned your studying went better today?"

"Yes," she agrees, but doubtfully.

"So you'll remain here, and buy things for the next week." It's a statement of fact, not a suggestion.

"I don't want to be excessive." She shifts uncomfortably.

"You won't be." And I really wish she would. I'd be delighted. "What do you need?"

She shrugs. "Just the stuff from my apartment."

"No. If they've put any tracking devices onto your possessions—they said they'd know if you contacted your parents, correct?—they could be monitoring you. Anything you need, I'll buy."

Anything she wants, I'll give to her if she asks.

Stupid moral code, it has never appeared before. I should push her down on this sofa, hold her still, and take what I want.

"I have to study properly." Her chin tilts up, resolute. "I have to do well in my exam, so I graduate with a degree. My parents think that's important. So, I'll need my laptop."

"A new laptop then. Done." That was easy. "What else?"

"Toiletries. Shampoo, that sort of stuff."

"Yes. We'll arrange that."

"And a few more clothes?" she says tentatively. "It's only a week, but..."

"Obviously." If she thinks this is putting me off, she's got another think coming. I'm delighted by the opportunity to spoil the woman I've been wanting. "Anything more you'd like?"

"And..." She bites her lip, clearly thinking about something she imagines I won't approve of.

"Go on." My heart thuds.

Say that you want me to lick your pussy for my every meal and as a midnight snack, I beg her mentally. That would be a delicious treat for me, as well as very relaxing for her. Perfect sustenance. I stare into her brown eyes, attempting to transmit the thought.

Ask for oral sex.

She gulps, and licks her lips, and for a second I think I've cracked telepathy and she's going to ask for another kiss.

"Books."

Nope. I'll try harder next time.

"I have some hardback editions of my favourite books. And I have an eReader."

"Of course." I remain impassive, and as we regard each other, I fight the urge to laugh, like we're teenagers playing a game of chicken. "And paperbacks? Those too?"

Her mouth twists into a reluctant smile. "They're kinda emotional support books."

"Can't survive without them." I'm going to spoil her with all the emotional support books she can cope with. She'll be so well supported she'll have the foundations of a skyscraper and reach as high.

She smiles shyly.

"Any jewellery?" I enquire.

That she dismisses with a quick shake of her head.

Pity. I have a particular piece in mind. But she didn't say *I* can't buy her an outrageously expensive diamond ring.

It's a simple plan: now I've saved her and got her with me, I will spoil her, take revenge against her enemies, and keep her.

Ideally, she'd fall in love with me too, and ask to stay. Otherwise, the day of her exam is going to be a disaster...

8

CATERINA

There's definitely something strange about the pictures Brody shows me. For the last week, when Brody arrives back after his workday, he presents photographs of a man or two who aren't either of the ones who attacked me.

My bruises have healed. But along with my growing affection for Brody—okay, love it's love, I'm stupidly in love—there's also fear that I have been putting off acknowledging.

But the trepidation is there. The suspicion prickles my spine with each photograph and online search. I've been living this odd sort of life where Brody is just my excessively-kind and generous landlord, who hasn't touched me since the night he kissed me and made me come, but who sets me aflame with every look.

And sometimes I catch him regarding me too. He turns when he realises, but he's incredibly attentive. The tension between us is stretching out, an elastic band about to snap.

I'm beginning to see a twist of impatience in Brody's expression now when he takes back his phone, as though he's frustrated.

I don't ask who the men are. But I am starting to wonder. I said yesterday that he can send me a photo during the day if he wants to. But he just shook his head, curtly.

Brody is gentle, respectful, generous, and if not exactly sweet, then... Not the thunderstorm I assumed he was. Obviously, he has a constant personal rain cloud above his dark hair. He still hasn't smiled. But he appears to enjoy our evenings together, and sometimes lingers in the morning over breakfast as though leaving is a struggle.

He wouldn't be looking for the men who hurt me, would he? He's a landlord, not some vigilante. But why do the photographs show men with closed eyes?

It's a crazy thought, but when Brody looks down at me and his phone is in my hand with another picture of a man, I can't help wondering... Who's the more dangerous predator? The men I hid from, or the man who found me?

There are other constants in the last week. Brody's chef and housekeeper, Denis, makes the most amazing food. Turns out, revenge pizza really isn't even his best dish. My mother is a great cook, but my god, I've never eaten so well as I have staying with Brody.

I think about my parents, but I don't get in contact for fear of putting them at risk. I feel safe here, in Brody's penthouse, in a way that's difficult to explain.

Brody doesn't touch me, and though I long for him, I press my lips together when I want to ask him to. He watches me closely, but he doesn't suggest anything. We spend evenings chatting over dinner, or rather, I talk, and he listens and asks occasional questions.

The evening before my exam, I should be nervous about that test. But I'm not. My mind keeps drifting to tomorrow, and that I'll have to leave the man I am now completely in love with.

I'm an idiot, because he's not just a landlord, even I can tell that. I think I can, anyway.

But despite his seriousness, he's, one, incredibly sexy. My body responds whenever he's close, tingling and heating. And two, very sweet.

Case in point, he walks in as I'm tying myself in knots about all things exam and future, sets a gold-edged paper bag onto the table before me, and stands back, hands in pockets.

"You can have the emotional support books if you've bought enough clothes," he states.

"Brody!" I laugh, but he remains stoic.

This has been an ongoing argument between us. He's really intent on caring for me, to the point of obsession. And I want to earn his approval, so when he scowls because I haven't replaced literally every item I own with a nicer version purchased with his credit card and delivered to the penthouse with baffling speed, I promise to do better the next day.

Except, of course, tomorrow there won't be a next day, and I have all these feelings built up. I swore I'd be braver, bolder after what I'm now calling the wardrobe-incident. Equally, I'd rather not humiliate myself by revealing how much I want Brody, when he has been kind in a doting uncle way. I still flush with embarrassment whenever I remember how I asked him to kiss me, and everything that happened afterwards.

So... All the time? Because I relive that memory a lot.

"Can I have a look before I prove I behaved?" I ask, half serious.

He nods soberly. "As long as you're telling me the truth.

I peek into the bag and gasp. They're the most gorgeous leather-bound, gilt-edged editions of my favourite romance series. His gaze is heavy on me as I draw out all six volumes.

"My god," I breathe.

"Do you like them?" He still has his hands shoved in his pockets as though he's enduring this.

"I didn't own any of these books in hardback." But I'm stroking their beautiful covers like they're my pets now. The only way he'd get them from me is by suggesting I stroke him instead. I wish he would.

"Oh well," he says deadpan. "They're good luck books."

Ah. Yeah. The exam. This is our last night together. And given my plan to find my parents is as ill-formed as two-year-old sticky tack, I'm going to make it count.

"Thank you." I tear my gaze away from the stunning books and get caught in his even more gorgeous eyes. Those colourless eyes that always seem to hide a rainbow of emotion.

"Now, your side of the bargain, moya koshechka." Is it my imagination or is his voice huskier than usual?

When I return from my bedroom wearing the little white sundress I bought for my exam tomorrow, he's lounged like a big black panther on the seat, a glass of whisky idly in his fingers. The drink is new, and his expression is dark. But his eyes eat me up.

He's silent as I spout nonsense about the fabric and the cut of the dress. But that's normal. I lapse into silence.

"And the rest?" he growls.

"That's it."

His mouth twists with dissatisfaction. "That's not enough dresses."

"It's plenty! I... I'm leaving tomorrow, remember?" The words stick in my throat.

He narrows his eyes, apparently ignoring my statement

about going. "I think you need more. And you didn't buy another bikini."

"What would I need with the one bikini you already bought me, never mind two?" He insisted I buy a bikini, and I don't get it. Honestly. He seems to believe I require an excessive number of clothes and books. It's bizarre.

"To use in the pool," he says, as though it's obvious.

"There's no swimming pool in this building's gym." I know. I went to the gym precisely once when I first moved in, checked out all the clean and tidy facilities, did twenty minutes on the treadmill, then couldn't walk properly for a week afterwards. Lesson learned. I'm not a gym bunny.

"I suppose you'd call it a large hot tub on the deck, not a swimming pool," he acknowledges.

My eyes go wide. I've been out onto the balcony. There's a stunning view of London, lush banana plants, comfy recliners. But no pool. "You have a hot tub?"

He inclines his head. "I'll show you."

9

BRODY

I'm not sure how Caterina avoided finding the stairs up to the little extra roof garden, but I suspect she's been creeping around rather than understanding that this is her permanent home now. With me.

She gasps as she precedes me onto the smaller upper level and sees the small inset infinity pool with a view over London. It's lit from below and gleams like a sapphire. The palms on the lower deck have lights shining up through their leaves, giving the impression of being above a jungle. Behind, the London night is a velvet black drape scattered with twinkling gems.

"This is amazing!" She grins, and that's more inspiring than the night sky.

"I'm glad you think so."

"Can I use it?"

"Come here," I order, and her obedience is another twang of my heart.

This. Girl. She could break me.

I touch her chin and turn her head side to side, examining her injuries carefully. I brush her hair aside to check the cut on her forehead, but it has healed nicely, and I can't resist smoothing my finger down her face. I imagine when there are just faded scars, how I'd love to splatter her pretty face with my come.

"I think you're healed enough. You can use it anytime you want."

"You're too good to me," she whispers, and those liquid chocolate eyes grab me by the throat again. She has no idea. Neither about how I am not a good man, nor the terrible, beautiful, sinful things I'd die to do to her.

"Will you come in too?"

Oh god, she's playing with fire. Swallowing hard, I give a single nod.

Caterina in a bikini? I'm there. Would I like to see her naked again? Yes. Absolutely. The image of her coming as I licked her has been tattooed onto my eyeballs since. I can't think of anything else.

I can't do anything but want her, and seek revenge against the men who hurt her. It's my obsession.

"What about now?"

Inwardly, I groan. "Da."

"Yay!" She skips back down the steps to change, and I follow with a sense of foreboding mixed with elation.

I'm quicker to swap into swimming shorts, and grab a couple of towels and a bottle of water, than she is to get changed, and I ease into the hot tub to wait. There's the muffled sounds of the city drifting up, but the air is balmy and the water warm, and the only thing that keeps me from relaxing is that tonight is Caterina's final night here that she's not aware she's a prisoner.

That and the fact I still haven't found the men who hurt her. My second-in-command is following up some leads, and the London Mafia Syndicate have been helping, but

I'm increasingly frustrated with the lack of progress. Admittedly, that hasn't helped the perception of the Syndicate that I'm trigger-happy.

Footsteps pull my attention away from that danger towards another. Caterina steps up to the pool in a bikini so cute and sexy I grip the tiles where my arms are laid over the edge.

"What do you think?" she asks, pushing one hip to the side and catching a fingertip between her teeth coyly.

I think she looks like temptation incarnate. Her young body is smooth and gorgeous, and my cock rises immediately. If I really were an angel, I'd fall from heaven to have her.

"I'm not sure. Buy a few others, and show me, then I can decide."

She huffs with laughter as she slips into the heated water and groans.

"That's so good." Rolling her shoulders she does a few laps of the small pool and I watch on indulgently.

"It's a hot tub, moya koshechka. You're allowed to relax," I say eventually.

"I know." She swims past me close enough to feel the water move with her kicks. "But it's been ages since I've swum. And it's deliciously warm."

"You're a tropical cat, mm? Don't get dehydrated," I say mildly.

"Oh!" She stops at the shallow end. "Have you got water?"

I pick up the bottle to bring to her, but she's already stepping across the pool. But she's short, and it shelves steeply—specially built because I'm oversized and was bored with shallow pools—and she nearly sinks her head below the surface of the water.

I've lunged and wrapped my free arm around her before I can think, and I tug her to me. Safe. My precious little cat. Not even the smallest harm will befall her, including getting that almost-healed wound wet.

She grasps my shoulders for support as she giggles and splutters.

"Whoops! That was deeper than I expected. Thanks."

And then, simultaneously, we both realise that in grabbing her up to stop her from slipping below the surface of the water, I've pressed her to me. All the way down our torsos.

My hot, erect cock is a steel bar against her thigh.

We both freeze. Pleasure throbs through me from where we make contact even as I know this is wrong. She's too young. Too sweet. My unwitting captive.

"Brody..." she whispers.

I bite back the instinct to tell her to ignore it, or that she doesn't have to do anything. Because instead of being repulsed, as she ought to be, she's leaning closer. And then I'm in a heaven I don't deserve, because she's looking up at me with trusting brown eyes.

"I want to..."

I ease backwards and slide the water bottle onto the side of the pool. And while I don't let her go—I'm telling myself it's so she can find her feet at the edge—I wait patiently. Alright, not patiently. Inside, I'm burning.

But I allow her to take her time, settling onto her own feet again and then running her hands over my naked chest, exploring the dip of my armpit and smoothing the hair that covers my pectorals. I bite back a groan as she follows that thin trail of hair all the way to the waistband of my shorts.

"I want to do for you what you did for me," she

murmurs, looking down and her cheeks pinkening. Shy creature. She's adorable.

"What do you mean?" I don't jump to any conclusion, even though we're pressed together. I'm primed to lift her out of the water and take her down to my bedroom, remove that tease of a bikini, and make her come with my cock. Chlorine scent and all, I'd love that.

"Putting my mouth on you."

Okay, I'm going to pass out and drown. For a second, I envisage her on her knees before me. I see her tears as I fuck her throat. I can almost feel her hair in my fist.

"Here," she adds. "I want to do it here."

Then, I remember where we are.

In a rooftop *pool*.

"Maybe not advisable. I'm in favour of you not drowning."

"You could sit on the side. Like when you put me in a chair."

I didn't think my cock could thicken any further, but that shows a pitiful lack of imagination on my part, because I'm painfully hard—and so sensitive that the brush of my shorts as I slip them down and the water swirls around my length—now she's suggested this.

She watches, curious, as I discard the wet shorts and in one smooth movement jump onto the side of the hot tub.

When the water is tranquil once more and I'm sat, my cock jutting upwards, Caterina approaches as though mesmerised. A little needy whimper escapes her as she fits herself between my knees, and she touches my cock tentatively, running one finger down the length.

"That won't all go in my mouth." She looks up at me, a bit afraid, half laughing, and pressing her thighs together so her hips move sensuously.

"It will if you want to try." And goddamn, that would be a gift I'd never forget. "But it doesn't need to," I reassure her. "You can use your hands too."

Her next touch is just as cautious, as though she might hurt me. Or perhaps that I will bite her.

"You're beautiful," she whispers reverently as she lowers her head and plants a soft kiss on the tip.

"Not as beautiful as you, doing this."

"Brody..." She strokes up my shaft experimentally, then her eyebrows pinch together. "You need to guide me..."

"I don't think I do, moya koshechka." I love seeing her puzzle out what to do. Her innocence is a delicate aphrodisiac compared to the savage turn on of the fact she wants to suck my cock.

"Teach me."

Her request hits me like a blow to the chest. This is her first time. It's a privilege and a responsibility. There's something special about novelty, and my cock throbs with it. Her pretty mouth has never had another man near it and she's mine to claim. I'm the one who will determine how she remembers this.

"Think of the top as like your clit."

She tilts her head, intrigued, then lowers her gaze, her long dark lashes fanning her cheek. Tentatively, she kisses the tip of my cock, and it twitches at the open-mouthed softness, and I let out a hiss. It wasn't much, but it doesn't have to be with Caterina. Just the sight of her is enough.

The next kiss sets up a flow of pleasure, and each one builds my arousal.

Her tongue circles around the tip. I gasp then groan as she becomes bolder, and tries to take more.

I wish I could be relaxed about this, but Caterina makes me crazy.

Her brown gaze fixes on me, seeking approval as she opens her lips and tentatively fits the helmet of my cock into her mouth. So gentle, but I groan.

"Like that?" She's slightly unsure.

"Deeper," I say hoarsely.

There's a glint of determination as she takes more, and the roof of her mouth brushes over where I'm most sensitive. She eases back, then down again, still so careful.

"Cover your teeth, but you can be firmer."

As her confidence increases, she takes me deeper and faster, and I lose all sense of reality that isn't this woman, and how well she does this, innocent as she is.

She's right. This is the perfect place.

Her head is the perfect height, and sitting at the edge of the pool has additional benefits. Men pretend they love standing to fuck a woman's mouth, and sure, it's nice. But Caterina is something totally different. She's a queen. I don't mind admitting that the thought of her on me is enough to make my knees go weak. And I have a feeling that coming in her soft, wet mouth will destroy me. Utterly.

And best of all?

It's entirely private, and yet I'm having a blow job from the most beautiful girl in the world, above all of London. The night sky is purple and orange, but I don't care that there aren't many stars because I have the light of my life standing before me.

I swell in her mouth, and she tries to swallow more of me, even though her eyes water and she chokes.

"That's it. My good girl."

I smooth my hand over her soft hair. I'm going cross-eyed with how well she's doing this. She's challenging herself, I can tell. And the feeling of the back of her throat on the tip of my cock? Fuuccccckkk. She's amazing.

Looking away isn't an option. I can't, and yet seeing her hair come loose as she bobs her head, willing and beautiful and *mine* drives my orgasm forward with embarrassing speed.

"I'm going to come in your mouth." I don't know if it's for her information to prepare her, or a promise.

She makes a sound of assent.

It's ecstasy as I come in long reams, pulsing, and I hold her gaze.

"Swallow." The demand is there before I can think that it's not within the rules I set.

And she does.

Her throat bobs as she accepts my come, her cheeks bulged with it. Then she raises her head and a line of spit dribbles down her chin. She's ruined. Perfectly, sweetly, used.

I reach down, grab her under the armpits and pull her up into my arms. Fuck my rule. She started it, and I'm going to make her come too. I need to. Settling her on my lap, I run a possessive hand over her arse, squeezing.

"Are you happy now I'm destroyed, moya koshechka?" I slide my hand down her wet belly and into her bikini.

"Yes." She grins wider, and her joy is so infectious that even I catch it as I sink my fingers between her folds and find her heated and slippery. Not water, here. No. That's arousal. Giving me a blow job has made my girl horny. And I suppose this episode has made me weak, because at the feel of her wet for me, my cheeks crease with a smile.

"Oh!" Grasping my thigh, she blinks with surprise, then gasps as I push one finger into her tight, slick heat. "Wow!"

"Everything alright?" I smirk as I rub my thumb over her clit. She's so responsive. She's soaked my fingers with her juices, and I'd lick her if I didn't want so much to see her face close to me as she comes.

"I joked to myself," she breaks off to moan as I begin to fuck her with that one finger, finding the right place on her inner wall and stroking that and her clit together. Her breathing goes ragged, and she squirms. "It would take an earthquake to make you smile."

The laugh is out of me before I can stop it, and she whimpers, flitting her gaze over my face.

"It did," I tell her softly as she shakes in my arms. "You're a force of nature. You're more powerful than you'll ever know."

And then I watch her face with the same satisfied smile, as I hold her on my lap and make her come all over my fingers.

She collapses onto my chest as she orgasms, and I nuzzle her dark hair and feel her pulse against my hand. She's sated and rests for a long moment.

"Oh my god, that was amazing." Lifting her head, she meets my eyes. "Though I meant for that to be for *you*. To say thank you for everything."

The chill of the night air finally cuts into me.

"You've been so kind," she continues, and that radiant smile is now shadowed. "I wanted to give you back a small part of what you gave me before I leave tomorrow."

"No need for that," I reply, my voice like a boulder rolling over my brittle hopes that she would come to care for me.

Obviously not.

Tomorrow she's going to discover that I won't let her go.

I have no intention of letting her leave, but it's better not to panic her yet. She's young and beautiful and innocent. I'm old and grumpy and savage. After her exams, the excuse can be the leader of the Italian mafia, who I haven't found yet. After that, I'll... I'm not sure yet. I'll set fire to her apartment if that's what it takes to have five more minutes with her with me.

"But it was," she insists. "And now I'm in your debt again."

She only gave me that magical closeness to her as a goodbye gift. As a fucking *thank-you*.

"Not at all," I reply tightly. "And we'll discuss all that after your exam." Holding her to me, I stand and carry her over to where I left the towels, and dry her off carefully.

I don't want her gratitude, hot though that blow job was. Neither do I want to take her by force, hot though that game would be.

I want her to love me.

My plan is in shambles. She won't let me spoil her as she deserves, I still haven't found the svolach who hurt her, and the clock is running down. I'm not ready to admit that tomorrow she'll only be here because I'll be forcing her to be.

Fuck. A billion in the bank and I can't buy the one thing I really want. Caterina's love.

10

BRODY

She walks into the breakfast room in the morning wearing a white sundress and gives me a nervous smile.

"I'm ready for my exam." She takes her usual seat—at my side—and pours herself a cup of tea. She belongs here. It's obvious in her every movement. "And then I'll be out of your hair."

"You're not in the way," I rumble, even as I think back to last night, and her *thanking* me. Fuck.

"Liar." She shoots me a wry look and it occurs to me how she's not nervous around me anymore. That sunny smile isn't something to hide behind. "Anyway, I've decided that after my exam I'm going to get my passport from my apartment, and search for my parents. They said once they wanted to visit the Cayman Islands, so perhaps they're there."

"No."

Her hand stops with a cherry halfway to her perfect little mouth. "What do you mean, no?"

No, in so many ways, not least that is a terrible plan.

"You should wait for your parents to contact you, as

they asked." I'm close to finding them, although Caterina is right about the Cayman Islands.

But before I can think of anything rational to say, she shakes her head. "I'm not imposing on you anymore, or putting you at further risk from the mafia."

"Caterina. That's ridiculous, I'm—"

My phone trills with my second-in-command's emergency ringtone, stopping me mid-confession of I don't know what. That I'm the last person who fears a poxy mafia so small as to be fussing over her family's modest theft? That I'm in love with her? That I'm not letting her go?

Shit.

"You should answer that," she says, popping the cherry into her mouth and chewing, her gaze sliding from mine.

Not now. Please, not now.

Last night we were on the edge of something. But she's withdrawing, and although for an instinctive moment my hand twitches to grab her, I make a fist and remember my internal vow. No forcing or suggesting physical contact. She has to ask.

"This will only take a moment," I assure her, and she shrugs. Because for Bogdan, my second-in-command, to be using that call system, it must be something that I've told him is of utmost importance.

"Boss, I think I've found them," Bogdan says as soon as I answer. "The Geraci mafia."

Finally. The name of the mafia I will obliterate.

Then as Bogdan continues, my stomach bounces like a kangaroo on a trampoline. I'm so close to getting revenge on the Italians who hurt my girl. I can't pass up this opportunity for Caterina's safety, quite aside from my pride. But as Bogdan speaks, it's clear. It must be today, and it has to be me that deals with them. But I was planning to spend the day taking Caterina to her exam then dealing with the fallout afterwards. And I'm not leaving her alone and at risk for her exam, so that means I'm going to mess up the one thing that Caterina has been working towards for the last three years: her degree.

Bogdan outlines the situation and I give directions for what to do next.

"Everything okay?" Caterina asks as I end the call, and the weight of this settles onto my shoulders like a too-heavy bar in the gym, threatening to buckle my knees.

Who do I trust to look after Caterina outside of this building? Normally, I'd say my team, but Steve is still in the hospital, and I'll need my second-in-command to ensure my revenge goes smoothly. She'll be in an exam room full of students, none of whom I control. There are so many ways for this to go wrong, from someone pulling the fire alarm and dragging her off, to her being taken by a fellow student paid by the Geraci mafia at the end of the exam.

Clearly, she can't go to her exam. It's too high a risk.

The solution is unpalatable.

I need her to stay here.

"How important is your exam?" I know the answer though.

She tilts her head. "The last thing I heard from my parents was that they requested I finish my degree. For years, they've been telling me how I must go into business."

My heart sinks.

"I've been studying for this exam, and it's one exam between me and achieving a degree."

Very important. I nod. "You can't attend your exam."

"Why?" Her brows pinch.

I search for something better than, "Because I'm a mafia

boss who needs to kill the men who hurt you". "I don't think it's a good idea."

Her expression of confusion quickly morphs into indignation. "I've been working hard for that exam."

"I know." I really do. But I cannot risk her safety to anyone but me, or hidden here where she's been snug and secure. "If I offered you a job instead, would you stay here and not go to the exam?"

"Why?" Her eyes snap with suspicion. "What would you be doing?"

I remain silent.

"I haven't left this penthouse since you brought me here. Then last night, I tried to..." She shoves her plate away. It hits the cafetiere, which topples and cracks, spilling the last of the coffee onto the table. "Shit, I'm sorry."

"Don't worry, what were you going to say?" My heart races. Last night was, "Thank you and goodbye", wasn't it?

"Never mind," she says frustratedly, and dabs at the coffee ineffectually with a napkin.

"What did you try to do last—"

"That's not the point." She scowls at the broken glass, then tosses the cloth onto the coffee stain and turns back to me. "You're telling me I can't leave?"

I don't reply. I can't say the words.

Understanding creeps across her face in a mix of fear and awe and panic.

"You're not just a landlord, are you?" she says faintly.

"Nyet." I knew this would happen, eventually.

"You're a mafia boss."

"Of Angel." I intend that to be merely fact, but I'm proud of it, even though I don't show it in ostentatious ways. This territory is knitted into my soul as firmly as Caterina is. I spend my time either caring for my people or taking vengeance on those who dare to think that because I'm a shadow, that I won't mind if they try to take what's mine.

Her mouth opens in shock, and regards me, sweeping her pretty brown eyes over my body. I can almost hear the ticking of her brain as she adds up what she's heard about me.

"The Dark Angel lives in my building?"

"Why not?"

"I thought..." She swallows and wariness wars with experience on her face. "I don't know what I thought. Half of us in Angel doubt you exist. The other half think you aren't human."

There was a time when that was at least partly true. But over the last few years, knowing Caterina? She changed me.

I approach slowly and she leans back in her seat. I continue advancing, bracing one arm on the table, trapping her in. With the other, I take her little hand and place it onto my chest, under my lapel and on the cotton of my shirt, over my heart.

"I exist," I say softly. "And I'm very human."

The steady beat thuds on her palm as she leaves her hand there after I release it, her palm warming me, before she smooths from side to side, seemingly mesmerised as we look into each other's eyes.

I'm forty-two years old. I've taken lives, I've had women. But I've never been in love until I met Caterina, or felt this connected with another person until now.

"I'm being held captive." Her dark eyes flicker with something that could be annoyance, but also... I wonder if it's not. If it's curiosity. Perhaps even a bit of arousal, as her chest pinkens, contrasting against her white sundress.

"You're still in the same building."

"Prison," she points out. But although she rails against

me, she doesn't attempt to move. "I can't leave this penthouse. Thus, it's a prison."

"If you count something with a rooftop pool, a personal chef, a gym, infinite streamed entertainment, and any luxuries you wish for delivered, as a prison." With a man who will worship her and give her anything she asks for. If she just *asks*.

"You do if you're a *captive*." Such a sassy mouth now she's found it.

"You're being strongly *encouraged* to stay for your own safety and comfort," I growl.

"Lack of liberty equals captivity."

"Has being here been so bad?" She's a damn house-cat railing against walls that protect and coddle her. For ten days she's been utterly content, so far as I can see. "It's not like before this you left the building except to work or go to university."

"That's not the point," she says, pushing gently against my chest. I allow it, giving her the distance she's implicitly requesting. "I'm not your pawn, Angel."

That change, to calling me by my mafia territory name, hits me in the heart. I invaded her space, and she pushed me away. I think—I fear—I've lost everything I've built with Caterina.

"I want to go to my exam," she says clearly.

And I must extinguish the threat to her life.

"Fine." I straighten. "You want a test of your business studies? I'll take you to prove yourself to the richest businessmen in London."

11

CATERINA

The Dark Angel.

He's a legend in this part of London, and he's been living above me all this time.

The Dark Angel has a reputation, shall we say? He's ruthless, but a shadow. He makes snap decisions, in and out of situations in a blink. He's cold and calculating, and he leaves death in his wake. The kingpin of Angel doesn't ask questions, he judges. And no god can help you if the Dark Angel has decided you're not wanted in his territory. The only punishment is death. No one survives an encounter with the Dark Angel, it seems.

Except me.

The only thing that doesn't stack up here is that he's been so kind and attentive. I'm nobody.

Though there are whispers of the Dark Angel's compassion, too. Always whispers. No one has ever met him or seen him, but rumours abound of his cold fury when someone is mistreated.

And looking at the glint in Brody's grey eyes... I can

believe it. He's Angel? Yeah. It suits him better, to be honest.

I should ask him about what he means by having me meet the wealthiest men in London, but I don't. I gulp, and as he pulls his phone from his jacket pocket, all the time regarding me carefully, as though I might run away, I voice the question I've needed to know. Have to know.

"Why have the men in the photos got their eyes closed?"

"Do not ask questions you do not want to hear the answer to, moya koshechka," he advises quietly.

"I do want to hear," I insist. Because I'm brave now, aren't I?

Not brave enough to tell Brody how you feel, a horrible little voice in my head says. *Not brave enough to ask him for what you really want.*

Shut up. This is different, and serious, I tell the nasty voice. This is totally different to my crush gone wild and having fallen right into adoration of this darkly protective, dangerous, kind kingpin.

"Mm. I think you know why their eyes are closed." Brody types into his phone with more force than strictly necessary.

Okay, that's true.

Their eyes are closed because they're dead, I finally admit to myself.

"You're searching for the men who hurt me?" I ask instead.

"I work with law enforcement."

"Really," I say flatly. That doesn't feel likely somehow. He's far too sinister for the police.

"Yes."

Defiantly, I reach for my cup of tea, and our gazes meet.

A shiver of something hot and dark goes down my whole body.

"The police," I repeat, allowing my scepticism to show.

"Well." He tips his head to the side. "Law enforcement. Or rather, people who enforce the law."

"The actual law, or some made-up law?" What has been happening? I feel a bit nauseous.

He shrugs and takes a sip of coffee. "I don't see the difference. Laws are only rules we made up and think are right, with some extra paperwork. I don't like paperwork."

"That's why you won't let me go to my exam, right? Because you," I don't know how my stomach feels about this, "are going to kill the men who attacked me."

He nods, teeth clenched.

And just like that, the jigsaw assembles itself. I had all the pieces, but couldn't—no, didn't want to—put them into the picture I now have.

First someone tried to kill me, and I discovered my parents were involved with the mafia, and my mother escaped the mafia. Then my upstairs neighbour is a billionaire kingpin.

The Italian mafia who came after me invaded his territory and his building. That questions his power. They hurt his pride.

The fact it's me is irrelevant. I am a pawn, a captive in this game.

"You wouldn't have let me leave, even if I'd tried, would you?" I ask in a little voice.

"Nyet." His confirmation is immediate.

It seems I've been kidnapped.

I *allowed* myself to be kidnapped. Crept out of my hidey-hole when he coaxed me, and right into his arms. No even a token fight. Nothing. The realisation is a punch in the gut.

Here I was, thinking I was safe.

But no. I've put myself in a cage with a bigger, more fearsome, predator. A *Bratva kingpin*.

"And afterwards, when you've completed your revenge spree today, I'll be free." That makes sense.

"No," he states implacably.

Wait. What?

"But you'll have your vengeance." I don't understand.

"This is the henchmen that have been found." His eyes glitter cold as steel. "I still need to get the kingpin, and make him pay."

"But..." The single word is a protest on behalf of the lie I told myself, and I now recognise he never did anything but allow me to believe. "After that?"

"You're not leaving," he enunciates carefully. "You're *mine*."

12

BRODY

She hasn't said a word since my possessive outburst. I suspect she's in shock.

I think I might be too. When she kept saying that she was leaving, I lost control, but I can't bring myself to regret it.

I'm not letting her go. She can hate me, and think she's a captive, but I can't keep breathing without her.

To the point that I've put my mafia boss reputation on the line.

Caterina doesn't complain or ask anything as I say we're going to her exam, just following me into the elevator and to the car. I tell myself that I take her hand and entwine our fingers tight because I don't want her to escape, but I'm a fucking liar.

I want the closeness we had last night.

We arrive at the hotel in Lambeth that has become the unofficial meeting place for the London Mafia Syndicate.

This is not the first time I've called an emergency meeting. It's not even the first time within a month. And admittedly, I am on the verge of getting kicked out.

They were already annoyed at me for slitting the throat of a svolach man they were squabbling about who was going to kill, then trying to find the Italians has decimated the last bit of my patience. I got impatient with Marco Brent for not handing over more information. The damage to the floor from my shooting it—look, it was very restrained that I didn't actually shoot Brent—was totally fixable. Plus, the relationship between Blackstone and his "convenient wife" has reputedly been much better since that incident.

I did give myself a reputation for being more easily angered than is generally the case. Caterina's safety does that to me.

But while there was some understanding about my position when I was desperately searching for the men who hurt my girl, I have a feeling an emergency meeting to help her avoid an examination could be less sympathetically met.

There's a small group of mafia bosses and their wives, all atypically informal because of the late notice. Where the women usually dress up for the official meets, Jessa Lambeth is in jeans and has a baby on her hip. She appears to be in an intense discussion with the Blackstone kingpin and his wife about the sling Blackstone is wearing that contains a sleeping baby. Blackstone is holding his wife's hand, toying with her fingers and the casual intimacy hits me in the gut.

I want that with Caterina. Her hand in mine, our baby close by. *Our baby*.

There are still people arriving, but I don't wait. "Thank you for coming."

"Always," Westminster replies seriously, and a couple of the other men nod.

"Grant couldn't make it," Jessa Lambeth says breezily. "I came instead. Who's your companion, Angel?"

I feel Caterina jerk with surprise at me being called by my mafia territory.

"This is my captive, bane of my life, pet cat, and destroyer of my most treasured possession," I reply, nudging Caterina forward, but I keep her hand gripped in mine.

There's silence.

"Sorry about the coffee," Caterina mumbles, then glances around warily as she chuffs with nervous laughter. I suppose the London Mafia Syndicate are intimidating, even when half of them seem to be off duty.

"Was the treasured possession your cock?" The Mayfair kingpin, Artem Moroz, asks in Russian. He barely bothers to hide his smirk, and I glare at him.

"No," I return in the same language. "My sanity." Coffee is basically the same thing.

"Sounds like love to me," Jessa pipes up.

"Angel, are you not even going to fake that she's your girlfriend?" Rhys Cavendish asks wryly. "It is the Maths Club rule." He shares an intimate look with his wife and jealousy spikes down my spine.

I glance down at Caterina, who is biting her lip in a way that's ambiguous as to whether it's worry or holding back a smile.

"That was not an option," I reply with more diplomacy than I'm known for. "She's my *captive*."

"Captive." Westminster's face goes dark as a Russian winter.

"Sure," drawls Artem, outright amused now.

"He rescued me," Caterina interjects. My surprise must show on my face, because she adds, "I guess."

Westminster narrows his eyes. "What do you want our help with, Angel?"

"I need you to examine her." Which is probably the

most ridiculous thing I've ever said, and that includes the last ten minutes.

Every eyebrow in the room shoots to the ceiling.

"Not like *that* unless you want to die today," I clarify. "An academic test of her *Business Studies skills*."

"He won't let me go to my final university exam," she explains to the mafia bosses who look either alarmed or sceptical or both.

"You are fucking kidding me," Bethnal spits out, then turns on his heel and strides towards the exit.

"Where are you going?" Artem calls after him.

"I haven't got time for this," he snarls. "I've got a wedding to *ruin*."

"How intriguing." Westminster smiles down at his wife.

"I know we call ourselves the London Maths Club, but that is a joke. This is a mafia syndicate. You're aware of that?" Cavendish says cautiously. "And aware of what a joke is?"

"He means our legit businesses," Jessa Lambeth interjects before I can reply, and leans in towards Caterina. "What would you do if your cash cow wasn't performing?"

There's a beat of silence.

"Low growth, but high market share, so, I would look for an alternative, stable investment." Caterina's voice gets stronger at the end of the statement.

"Good answer. Is that why he kidnapped you?" Cavendish smirks. "The Bratva men have no head for numbers."

"I can count the number of men I've—" I snarl.

"Angel." Adi Cavendish slips in front of her husband and raises one blonde eyebrow pointedly. "I thought you said you had something you needed to do."

She has a point. The Geraci men who hurt my girl won't murder themselves.

"Fine. Proceed." Swallowing, I step back. I glare at the gathered mafia bosses over Caterina's shoulder. My hand is still gripping hers, and I'm sure for a second that she's holding on tight too.

"Will you be okay?" I lean down and say into her ear.

She turns her head, and her mouth is close enough to feel her breath. Her brown eyes are too near to see clearly. I wish fervently that I had the right to kiss her.

I'm breaking all my rules as it is.

"Yes," she whispers.

"You're going to do great," I reply, almost against her lips, then withdraw. "Don't let her leave. I have something I need to do. I'll be back," to claim Caterina, "as soon as I can."

I arrive at the normal-looking townhouse and take the steps at a run. Bogdan meets me at the door.

"We have them."

"I thought you said this was going to need all our resources?" I scowl, but follow as Bogdan leads me into a room where two cowardly excuses for men are tied to spindly chairs.

The fury explodes in me like flame held to gas. They hurt Caterina. They terrified her. If it weren't for her quick thinking, they would have killed and defiled her in the most horrific way.

I snatch my gun from its holster and the world slows and narrows to pulling back the safety and feeling the ricochet as I fire again and again through the red haze until I'm squeezing the trigger, but nothing is happening.

I've emptied the clip.

They're dead and I have to shoot them more.

Again. I'd resurrect them to murder them again, and again.

I'm breathing heavily, as though I've run a mile at a sprint. They're done. This has to be enough.

It's not.

A few steps and I'm punching first one then the other across their bloodied faces, time after time. I beat them until my arm tires, and I step back. They're unrecognisable.

"And this," Bogdan says dryly from beside me, handing me a cloth that I take a second to realise he means me to clean my knuckles with. "Is why we interrogated and photographed them before Angel arrived."

It's only then that I notice I'm surrounded by a dozen of my best men. They waited for me. I catch more details then. The coverings on the floor. The video camera set up to the side. A pile of handwritten notes.

Bogdan knew I would lose my cool.

I take a deep breath and am shocked to find it's shaky in a way I've never been before. I clean my hands and check my suit before tossing the cloth away. Killing men who deserve it doesn't bother me, but the importance of revenge for them touching Caterina rocked me.

"Did you get the information?"

"Da. The Geraci kingpin is as good as dead."

"Good." The calm settles onto me, a heavy blanket.

Now to return to what really matters: moya koshechka.

When I get back, Caterina, far from being grilled, is lounging in a comfortable chair, sipping a drink, and chatting with Jessa Lambeth.

"The business strategy for my interior design company differs from what I do for Lambeth," Jessa is saying, and I pause to watch.

Caterina has charmed them all, of course she has. She didn't know it, but these are her people. I intend to keep my distance for a few minutes, but as though she feels the connection between us too, Caterina turns and sees me. And sweet as it is to regard her, the hint of a smile when our gazes meet is pure sugar.

I'm at her side in an instant.

"Did she pass?" I ask Jessa abruptly, not taking my eyes off Caterina.

"Yes, and—"

"Good. Because I have something I want to discuss with my captive."

Caterina blinks. "I'm enjoying myself."

I have no patience for this. I need to have her alone. I lean down, and whisper into Caterina's ear. "Don't make me toss you over my shoulder, moya koshechka."

She gasps. "You wouldn't."

And that's where she's totally wrong, because I grab her up, and holding her sweet thighs, carry her out with her cute butt close enough to kiss when she pummels my back.

It's not kidnap. It's love.

13

CATERINA

He puts me down into the back seat of a car and slides in beside me, cool as you like.

Everything I thought I knew about Brody has been turned upside down today. I don't know what to think.

Sliding his phone from his pocket wordlessly, Brody hands it to me.

On the screen are two men side by side. Eyes closed. My body knows what this is before my brain does, and I'm shaking. I try to form words, but I can't. I just nod.

The men who came after me, who would have done terrible things to me, are *dead*.

Brody clasps my cheek, tips my face up, and frowns.

I didn't stop this, and I probably could have. I could have told Brody no more. I let this happen, and all I can think is how scared I was when they invaded my home and threatened my family. Does it make me an evil person that I'm not sad they're dead?

I'm overwhelmed with emotions I can't name.

How does it reflect on me that when Brody said the

others deserved it too, and I shouldn't mourn the men whose closed eyes I've seen, that I believe him?

I want to trust him.

I don't want to leave. But he has to want me.

"Oh Caterina." He sighs and plucks the phone from my hands and tosses it away, before gathering me into his arms. "Don't cry."

I didn't realise I was, but I give in to it, pressing my face into the warm, deliciously-scented ocean-and-steel softness of his grey shirt. The emotions of today—and since the day I discovered I was a mafia target—are too big.

Relief. So much relief I'm almost drowning in it. It's only letting it go that I recognise how tense I've been. Everything from the attack in my apartment and the fact the men were still out there, uncertainty about my parents, worry about my last exam, and the halting dance of attraction and suspicion with Brody has been weighing on my mind. Now the men are dead, the London "Maths Club" gave me a Business Studies examination much tougher, but funnier and more engaging, than the essay questions I was expecting, and something has changed between Brody and me.

Too tired to argue, I accept his guidance. He lifts me out of the car with his hands under my knees and at my back, carrying me. So long as I can keep my face glued to his chest, I don't care. Maybe I'm beyond pride now, because I don't question that there's a helicopter, and he gently but firmly straps me in and puts ear defenders on me, my legs still over his thighs and my shoulders nestled close.

Somehow, I must sleep, or rest, or something, because when I next open my eyes, it's quiet and I'm surrounded by Brody's solid, comforting presence.

"Hey," he murmurs, brushing a wisp of hair from my cheek and looking down at me with a soft smile.

"Hey." I totally broke down there. Ack, I'm embarrassed and try to sit up. Brody's grip on me tightens for a moment, as though to stop me, then immediately loosens.

"Where are we?" We're on the ground, on a large, neat, green lawn. That's why it's quiet. Brody lifts off my ear protection and his, and I manage the adult feat of unbuckling myself and standing up. Well done, me.

"You seemed to need to be out of the penthouse in London, so we're at my home in Yorkshire." He lifts me out of the helicopter, nods to the pilot who apparently had been waiting for me to wake, because once we're clear, he takes off, leaving Brody and me together holding hands as we walk across the manicured lawn towards a huge manor house.

"This is yours?" I ask in disbelief. I guess I shouldn't be surprised, but while my parents aren't poor, they are nowhere near the "kind of place people visit for picnics and tours" level.

He nods.

It's a castle. It's amazing. The creamy yellow stone is aged and worn, there is a plant climbing all over one half, the pink flowers like cupcake sprinkles. Over the porch entrance there's a riot of peachy roses. It's unspeakably lovely.

And maybe it's his intention, but I'm utterly distracted. Was I annoyed with him? Was I upset? Maybe. I can't remember what about. Who cares when my heart lifts as he leads me through the gardens towards the house.

"It looks very grand and old." And I feel both charmed and rather out of place.

"Twelfth century, I believe, though no one really knows." It's only then that I notice he hasn't let go of my hand. His long fingers are laced with my smaller ones. He's so tall my forearm is parallel to the ground. "There are historic parts of the house, especially the cellars."

"Has it been in your family all that time?"

"Nyet." His mouth twists as he glances across at me. "My family comes from Russian peasant stock. Nothing grand about the Marchenkos, but we know how to make revenge pizza, and it's almost dinner time. Denis has been hard at work in the kitchen today."

And suddenly, I know where this is going. More evasion. No answers, no clear understanding of how he feels or what he wants. If I allow him, before I know it, he'll have an eminently-sensible reason I should stay here for my safety or comfort, and I'll be as confused as before.

I adore this man, but I deserve more.

I halt, as we reach the edge of the formal flower beds that surround the house, digging my heels in when he tugs my arm.

"Moya koshechka?"

"Why have you brought me here?"

"You said you wanted to leave London," he replies calmly. "I thought a change of scenery would be helpful."

"No."

He raises his eyebrows. "No?"

"That's nonsense." I take a deep breath. "You've asked me what I want, and given me gifts—"

"Those were—" he rumbles.

"Brody." Impatience licks at me as surely as the afternoon sun. I don't allow myself to second-guess this. He enjoyed it last night in the pool, I know he did. But for some reason, he won't do anything about it. "What do you want with me?"

He stares down at me silently, mouth in a flat line.

"You said I couldn't leave. Does that mean that you want *me*? Because you've had plenty of opportunities, but you haven't touched me."

He straightens to his full, imposing height and his jaw clenches.

"Tell me, or I'll escape." I throw out the threat desperately.

"I'll find you," he replies.

"I'll escape again."

"Wherever you run to, Caterina." He draws my hand inexorably towards him. His voice is husky. "I will find you and bring you home."

Ohh. Oh my god. It takes all my effort to not melt. The idea of him coming for me, wherever I am? Scorching.

And I smile. Because it's not a confession of love, but it might as well be. Still, I need more. "I'll run at every opportunity. You'll be forever dragging me home."

His silver eyes gleam in the afternoon sunlight. "That's not such a terrible game."

My heart thuds. But in a good way. With excitement, like I'm glad to be alive. "Okay."

"Okay," he repeats cautiously, sober again. He's sceptical. Wary. My grumpy Bratva kingpin is worried I'll reject him, I realise. In some ways, he's as scared as I was when he pulled me out of that wardrobe. And as lonely.

"Chase me." I'm throwing in all my pride here. Maybe it was the bruised and battered girl who he didn't fancy, but I'm healed now, and I have to try. "I'm going to run. If I can get away, you'll tell me what you want." I leave the implication hanging. I'll come back.

"My little cat," he says, voice soft and smoky, a smile curling over his lips. "If you win, I'll tell you *everything*. I'll tell you my every sordid desire. I'll tell you things that will make you blush like fire."

I'm already nodding. "Yes. And then I can choose, and you'll let me go if I wish."

"But if I catch you, I'm going to *do* whatever I want, for as long as I want. I get to keep you." His voice has lowered further. It's pure sex.

My nipples think so too. And my pussy. They both zing.

"You need proof of how much I crave you, moya koshechka? You need to be hunted and captured?" A hint of a smile tugs at his mouth.

The sound that comes from my throat is one of agreement, but it's of a small, soft prey animal. My breath is all shallow and my heart is racing already. Yes, yes.

What will he do when he catches me? If I win, he'll tell me his desires, and my mind fills with delicious, filthy words that he could pour into my ears. Things I could respond "yes" or "no" to. Gifts to unwrap.

But if he wins... He won't tell. He'll show.

He'll claim whatever he wants. Since I've been his captive all he's ever done is what I asked. The reversal makes me quiver with anticipation.

I won't get a choice.

"Come." He turns us away from the house and leads me through the garden. The sun is lowering, gilding every surface with pink gold and casting shadows so dark you could fall into them.

It takes me a moment to see where we're going, then my heart ticks faster as we emerge from the long borders of flowers to the entrance of a maze.

"I will give you thirty seconds' head start," he says.

"Make it to the centre before I catch you, and I'll tell you everything."

"But you know the maze, and I don't," I protest. It's not fair in the slightest.

"I don't intend to lose, little cat." His eyes go like steel. "Run."

14

BRODY

Her eyes go wide, and she hesitates, like she's wondering what I'm going to do and she's not certain I meant it about a chase. I tug at my tie, and it slides off my neck, then I flick open the top button.

I absolutely meant it.

Fuck honour, and convention. Fuck the idea of giving her choices, as though I'm a polite British gentleman, and not a brutal Russian Bratva boss. What was I thinking? I've been spending too much time with the London Mafia Syndicate and their ridiculous, "Ask questions before murder" policy.

Fuck our age difference, and the fact she's a sunny little angel to my murderous darkness. Fuck the mafia responsibilities that kept me from her. Even fuck the rest of my revenge against the mafia who hurt her, if the price would be that she ever felt unwanted again. I allowed that insecurity to grown in her, when I should have been claiming her as my own and covering her with my seed day and night.

"Aren't you going to escape?" I taunt her. "You've been saying you want to leave. This is your last chance. Run." I keep my expression unreadable as I shrug off my suit jacket and flick off my cufflinks, allowing them to drop onto the growing pile of clothes at my feet. It doesn't matter. There's no one here but her and me. "I'll catch you either way."

Then her shoulders go back and the little fighter I know is there emerges. I smile as she turns on her heel and runs fast.

Adrenaline surges in me as I strip off my shirt. My shoes are utterly unsuitable for this activity, being leather and shiny, but it's irrelevant. I'll still win. Because what my girl doesn't realise is that I love her far too much to allow her to escape.

I finish the countdown in my head.

"I'm coming for you, Caterina," I call, then listen intently.

I hear light steps on the left side of the maze. She's soft pawed. Setting off at a run, I twist and turn through the paths. It's shadowed, and the bright sunlight and dark-green hedges make my fucking ancient eyes slow to adjust.

I can't quite figure out which route she took, so I pause.

"Little ca-at," I sing-song. "Where are you?"

She huffs a laugh. "As if I'd tell you."

My head flicks to the side. "Interesting. You're further through than I expected. Quick."

There's a muffled curse. "I won't be revealing my location again, Brody."

But she redoubles her pace, and I can hear her feet hit the compacted gravel harder now. It's too easy to lope through the maze after her. The scent of the box hedges is mixed with lavender and rosemary from the herb garden to the side, and I wonder if she can smell it too.

It's the sweet essence of home.

This will be where we live together, at least some of the

time. Where we'll raise our children and grow our influence.

Her steps halt, and there's the gritty sound of her feet twisting on the ground as she backtracks out of a dead end. The plan of the maze clear in my mind, I calculate where I think she is. Just a couple of hedgerows separate us, though I need to go around several loops to get to her.

"Moya koshechka."

She yelps with shock at how close I sound, and I chuckle.

"I'm getting to the middle first, Brody."

I hum thoughtfully as I speed up to a run, gaining on her even as I'm further away.

"Where are you?" she mutters.

"Don't worry, I'm coming for you." I accelerate, closing on her. "Enjoy your last taste of freedom, trapped in my maze, Caterina. Because when I catch you..."

She gasps.

"You're *mine*."

15

CATERINA

I sprint through the maze, thoroughly lost, and it's exhilarating. I'm not even trying to find my way to the middle, or out. I'm just trusting in luck.

After a lifetime of being a good, cautious girl, I'm turning this way and that, randomly. It wasn't so long ago that other predators were searching for me. I outsmarted and outlived those men, and was found by a bigger, scarier monster, who has revealed his possessive side.

The Dark Angel claimed me, just as he will now.

The afternoon air is warm and fragrant, and Brody's heavy footsteps are everywhere and nowhere. I've been running for a few minutes, or longer, I'm not sure. I try to keep track of the turns and the blind alleys as my chest gets tight and my muscles complain at the sudden exertion.

There's a sheen of sweat on my skin, and my feet slap the ground.

I feel like a maiden in the Minotaur's labyrinth, with a dark and dangerous creature behind me. Something forbidden. I'm still wearing my white sundress, and underneath are the lace knickers and bralette that Brody made me blush by opening in front of him. A virgin girl, lost.

The hedges on all sides are oppressive. Close. Wherever I look there's densely-packed small green leaves. Except, in some places, as I've progressed into the maze, the sunlight doesn't reach fully, and there are thinner patches where a peek of the other side is possible.

I come to a fork where one path is only a couple of paces before another turn. The shadows are deep, the sun only slicing across the top of the hedge. The other, soft orange-yellow light blazes down towards me before it curves away.

"Caterina." Brody's voice is close enough to startle me.

The decision paralyses me. Light? Or dark?

"Are you near the centre?" His tone is teasing, and through a thin hedge, I see movement. "Does my scared little cat not want to feel what I'll do to her pussy?"

I bolt. Not for the sunshine, but into the dark, where the path twists and turns back on itself, until I'm running down another path, shorter this time.

Either way, I win, right? Because Brody—the Dark Angel—is coming after me. He's near. I can hear his footsteps at a controlled but rapid pace. He had a smouldering fire in his silver eyes when he told me to run, and whatever the result of our chase, I intend to discover what happens when that flares into life.

He's gaining on me.

Then I see it. A peek of light that is impossibly low on the hedge. That pattern of gold can only come from a break in the maze's pattern. The middle.

I ease to a walk, unable to believe it. I'm going to win. A few more paces, and I'll turn the corner and Brody is too far behind me. He will have to be honest—

He crashes through the hedge from the side, and I shriek in fright, grasping for him even as I try to stop and pivot. Angel catches me around the waist, tight as I battle against him instinctively.

"I've got you, Caterina. You're *mine*."

16

BRODY

She squirms as I hold her to my chest. "That's cheating!"

"Da." I hoist her higher up my front, dragging her over my hard cock. "I'm a devious fucker. I will do anything to have you, Caterina. I would never let you leave, and I'm going to take everything I want. I'd defy every god. I'd fight death himself."

"Brody..." Her voice has gone disbelieving and soft.

One turn, and we're at the centre of the maze. The sunlight shines onto the circular wood and glass pavilion at its heart. It's a luxurious little space that I had planned to bring Caterina to visit tomorrow. I open the door with my elbow, and she gasps.

The single room is richly furnished as a relaxation snug and boudoir, with all the comfort you could possibly want. And thankfully all the preparations I ordered have already been done. There are clean white covers on the bed, champagne flutes on a side table, and candles ready to be lit.

I set her down onto the bed and stand back.

"Do you have any idea what a little temptress you are?"

I ask conversationally as I strip off the rest of my clothes, tossing them away.

She shakes her head, lines appearing between her eyebrows as she takes in my naked body.

"You're so big," she breathes. I glance down to where her gaze keeps returning. My cock is hard, red, veined, and throbbing. Not a surprise she's alarmed.

"Your little body will fit my huge cock, don't worry," I assure her, roughly palming my length and giving it a few long, lazy strokes. "And since you nearly got to the centre of the maze, I'm going to tell you what I want before I take it."

I insert one knee between her thighs, pushing her legs apart, and smooth the lines on her forehead away with my fingers.

"I'm going to claim you. I'm going to fuck you and breed you." A soft gasp reveals that's probably too much, but I don't care.

Tugging up her skirt, I groan as her little lace knickers are revealed. "I've stroked my cock to the image of you in that underwear every night since you showed them to me," I admit gruffly. She arches and wriggles to help me remove her dress, and fuck, her body is perfect.

"You're amazing," she breathes as her fingers reach up to investigate my chest, and creep downwards, making excitement spike at the base of my spine.

Her innocent curiosity threatens to derail all my plans.

"Not so fast, moya koshechka. I'm going to pleasure you first." I take her questing hand from my abdominals and put it over her head. Then because she whimpers in protest and her tits are so lovely in this position, I do the same with her other hand, so she's exposed.

"You belong to me, now," I tell her, trailing possessive fingertips down her front and over her belly to where her lace knickers are already soaked through. "I'll push into your hot little body, make you come on my cock, and then I'm going to fill you up with my seed until you're swollen with it."

Her eyes drift closed, and I grip her chin.

"Look at me."

And then her soft brown eyes open again, and she pants, her mouth a sweet and enticing "o".

I trace my fingers gently down her face. She tilts her head, revealing her tender, vulnerable neck.

"You're like a stray cat. All beautiful and wary, chirping for attention but not coming close enough to stroke. But now, moya koshechka, you're my pet. I'm going to collar you."

I suit my movements to the words, making my hand into a necklace that stretches nearly all the way around her neck because I'm so much bigger than her.

"I'll give you something to wear here, and a ring around your finger. A ring worth more than some countries' entire wealth to show you once and for all that you are precious to me. Far too important to allow you to stray from my control." I tighten my grip on her throat the slightest amount, just enough to let her know I'm the one who holds her now. "Do you understand?"

"Yes." Her breathing is uneven, her pulse flutters, and as I cast my gaze down, I see her nipples clearly visible through that tease of lace.

"So will you be my good girl and not try to run from me again?" I can't live without her.

"Is that what you want?" she breathes.

How can she doubt that? "All I want..." I brush my hand down over the smooth skin of her clavicle until I get to the bralette. "Is you."

I cup her little breast and rub my thumb over the nipple, and she moans.

"So responsive. Such a good girl when you comply." Leaning down, I put my lips to her nipple, tormenting her with the soft wet of my tongue through the lace. "You're going to take my cock so well."

Hooking one finger on the strap of her insubstantial bralette, I drag it down, revealing the swell of her naked breast.

"So beautiful," I murmur before taking the tip into my mouth to suck. So fucking delicious, her skin is divine. She bucks as I nibble and take ruthless advantage, easing down on top of her and nudging her thighs wider. I continue to lavish attention on her sweet little breast before switching to the other one with a groan of pure desire as she squirms beneath me, unconsciously rubbing my erection on her thighs until it notches where she's soft and wet.

We both stop.

But for that scrap of lace, I'd be pressing into her. I'd be popping the sweet cherry of her virginity.

"Off." I'm grabbing at her knickers, and she wriggles as I shove them down her legs. "And that."

I gesture vaguely, but she understands and scrabbles to get her bralette off. I manhandle her into the middle of the bed and can't even stop to admire her naked body fully—I have to get my mouth onto that soaking little pussy of hers.

Holding down her thighs, I bury my head between her legs. There's no finesse or gradual build up this time. I part her lips and drag my tongue over her clit, the sweet and salt of her hitting like a drug.

She cries out, and I do it again, but more. Harder. I lick, and lick, gorging on her. I *need* this. And so does she, because it's only minutes and she's coming. She jerks and shudders and screams my name in a way that makes savage pride avalanche down from my heart to my cock, stiffening it more.

And when I lift myself up, I grin as I see that she's sweaty and electrified, not sleepy and sated.

"Is that normal?" she asks, reaching out for me, her chest heaving.

"It will be for you."

She laughs with delight, and it's the best sound in the world.

I sit back and pull her onto my lap, holding her tight, her arms draped over my shoulders, and kiss her deeply. My erection presses into her soft belly, and her breasts are squashed against the planes of my chest. Being skin to skin is everything I thought it would be.

For a while, I just hold her, keeping her close, and enjoying this moment. She's small and slight, but fits on my lap so easily, and our height difference means we're face to face. I breathe her in, kiss her neck, and savour the last moments of my girl being a virgin. Until she begins to squirm, arousal fully revived and impatience engaged.

"I'm going to put you onto my cock," I murmur, grip her hips, and drag her up my body until the soaked entrance of her pussy notches at my head. Any control or filter on my words or actions has gone. "I'll release my sperm deep inside you. I'm going to fill you up and get you pregnant."

I kiss her lips and shudder with pleasure at the promise of her wet heat.

"Yes," she says around my hungry kisses, her hands all over me. Stroking my upper back, pressing the muscles of my neck as she writhes on the blunt end of my cock. "Yes. Impregnate me. Give me your baby."

"I will." I can barely bring myself to let her go enough to

allow her to slide down onto where we both need her to be. "I'm going to breed you."

She lets out a little sob as we press together, gravity dragging her onto me. And despite her being my perfect virgin angel falling, she feels like heaven.

"Oh god, you're too big. I can't." She flexes up, but the protest is a lie, because she's already sinking back lower.

"That's it." Swapping into my mother tongue, I whisper into her ear. "My falling angel. My love. Moya koshechka, take more."

"It hurts," she whines, but not in a bad way. Breathless and needy, she pushes down another inch.

"You have a greedy little pussy. It will hurt until you're used to it." I hold still, even as my body throbs with the need to rut her. To mark her. I let her get used to my size. She shifts infinitesimally from side to side and up and down, and her tight, tight pussy gives.

"That's it. Open for me."

"You're splitting me apart. I've never..."

"I know." I soothe her. She's tiny, and I'm big. This first time for us was always going to be difficult. Fuck, she's squeezing my cock. She's incredible. "But I promise you'll love it soon enough."

"I already do," she insists. "I love that you're so close. That you're *in* me."

I can't speak to agree with her, because I'm choked with love and the feel of her tight passage sliding onto my cock further and further until we're joined fully and she's panting and wriggling on me, held by my arms.

She's mine. She'll never belong to anyone else. I've claimed her, and I'll make this so good she can't see anyone else. That completion of the beginning eases up my throat.

"You belong to me now, always." I press my cheek to hers as I pour the declaration into her ear. "I love you."

"I love you." She loses the words into my shoulder, but they make their way to my heart, anyway.

"Not half so much as I love you. You'll never doubt me again, I'll ensure it. I'll have you well fucked and in a constant state of ecstasy and contentment."

"I'm so glad you found me," she murmurs. "I needed you."

"I'll never let you go."

I relish her soft skin. Her pussy is the most amazing, sheath for my cock. She's silk and velvet clenching on my length. I grasp her little arse and lift her an inch, then slide her back down.

She moans.

"You like that, huh? You like your man's cock?" I don't need her to answer, because I can feel her whole-body shudders of need.

"I love it," she confirms anyway.

"You're so perfect." I push my fingers into her hair and pull her head back to bare her neck, then kiss her there as I flex my hips, fucking up into her in short, leisurely strokes. "I can't wait to see you lush and round with my child. You're going to be even more lovely when you're bred."

"Please," she sobs.

My slow pace is frustrating her, but I'm not ready for this to be over.

"Come for me. Two orgasms and I'll give you what you want, moya koshechka."

17

CATERINA

He crams his hand between us and finds my clit as though he knows my body better than I do. And my god, perhaps he does, because as he rubs me, I've never felt anything like it.

I've dreamed of being with Brody in this way from when he was just my neighbour, but the reality is simultaneously more intimate, sweeter, and filthy, in ways I didn't expect. Being on Brody's lap as he takes my virginity is empowering, as well as having an edge of him using me. He moves me for his pleasure as though I'm his beloved toy, to be played with and cherished. I might not be being ground into the mattress, but he's in charge, regardless of whether I'm laid out on the bed as his personal feast or being bounced on his huge erection.

All of these things are fantastic for me. Sure there was a twinge of pain as he breached my virginity, but now every part of where we're joined sparkles with pleasure.

"Come all over my cock like a good girl," he rasps. Then I just spy his sly smile as he bites my neck, and thrusts up—hard—from below.

I break apart with this second orgasm. It's an explosion as strong as an ocean wave. Brody holds me, soothing me as though I'm in pain as much as mind-bending pleasure.

He murmurs soft words in Russian and through the fog of lust and love, I realise that's his thing. He cares for me. This man looks after me as tenderly taking my virginity and making me come on his monster cock as he did when cleaning my wounds.

I try to say, "I love you," but it's all garbled and whimpers and I think sounds more like, "uhhh wub yuhh," and then disintegrates as another wave sweeps me away.

"I know, I know. You're beautiful as you come." He holds my head with a hand firmly in my hair as I crumple on top of him.

"I'm going to fuck you now, moya koshechka," he says into my ear. "I'm going to flip you onto your back and pound into you. I waited for you to ask, but now I'm going to have you."

"Uhgh—" I'm nodding but not capable of human language. My whole body is tingling.

"I want you to take every thrust like a good girl. I'm going to use you fast and hard, because you're *mine*."

"I belong to you." The admission comes out with an oof as I land on my back, Brody still inside me. "Yes." I stroke up and over his shoulders and shift my hips until he's even deeper. "Yes."

There's something dark and controlling that shudders down my spine as he removes my hands from his body one by one and holds them down with his own. As though my touching him will be too much. Withdrawing with a long, lazy stroke, he slams back into me, sending sparks of delicious sensation flying out from where we join.

"That's it, my good girl," he grunts as he rams into me

again. Then he sets up a confident pace, unrelentingly fucking me, as he kisses my lips and cheeks and I just melt. Or burn. I don't even know. I'm reduced to being his sheath and it's ecstasy with every stroke of him into me. As though we're making some new magic between us.

And of course, we are. We're creating a baby.

This man is all my dreams made real.

"Fill me up," I whisper, not quite believing my daring. I tilt my hips, and Brody nods and goes deeper still. "Make me yours forever, Dark Angel. Come inside me, my virile husband-to-be. I want a baby bump that shows everyone how you bred me. How I'm yours in every way."

He groans and thrusts even harder.

"You're a dream." His words are ground out. Hoarse. "I'll never stop wanting you. No one will touch you again without dying, because you belong to me. The sun will be cold before my love for you ceases. I don't care the price, Caterina. I'd pay it, anything. Every penny I have or will ever have. My heart, my soul, my life. Anything to keep you safe and happy. Nothing could be too much to own you."

"I'm yours," I echo. Because that sounds like the best thing. To be Angel's prized, loved, treasured possession. He certainly feels like he owns me as he pounds that thick length into me without mercy.

"You'll wear my ring. Have my children. Come on my cock." He punctuates each statement with a brutal thrust. It should hurt, but it doesn't because he's so deep in me he's rearranged my organs. The sensation of fullness is unbelievably good. "You're *mine*. I'll never let you go."

He's heavy on top of me, his weight a reminder of how big he is compared to me. He's powerful and large and savage, and yet even as he's taking his pleasure with my body, he's giving everything of himself. My Dark Angel is gradually losing control because of me.

"Moya koshechka." He says a deluge of words in Russian, mixed in with strangled praise and love in English. And my name. I'll ask, and I'll learn his language, but right now I don't need to know exactly what he means. I can hear the emotion. The love is in every gruff word and passionate touch. I know that he's pouring out adoration and obsession.

I open my legs wider and strain to dig my heels into his firm buttocks. We're connected as intimately as two people can be: him ramming into my body, and overflowing thoughts in my mind.

"Come inside me," I urge him. "Take what you need."

His hands tighten on mine, and he shudders. Then he lifts his head from where he was kissing me, and then he's scraping his gaze over my face before staring right into my eyes.

My heart balloons with love for this man, and as though he was waiting to be looking into me, Brody's movements go ragged. Those grey eyes of his shimmer with ribbons of colour in the low light.

His cock swells even more, before he thumps hard into me and stops, yelling out his release as he pumps wet heat deep in my pussy, right up against my womb.

To get me pregnant. To breed me, exactly as he promised.

For a second he has no control left, just collapsing, resting all that delicious bulky muscle of his body onto me. He presses me into the covers, his cock lodged all the way in, my legs wrapped tight around his waist. And the rumours are right. This man is the Dark Angel. That's the only explanation. He might crush me to death, but I don't care one bit. Being this close to him is everything I'll ever want.

He groans and rolls over scooping me with him until I'm laid half next to and half on top of him and we lie there, spent, our breathing gradually slowing to normal. Since I'm spread over him, his come seeps onto his thigh, and with a growl of disapproval, Brody pauses in caressing my waist and bottom, and reaches down between my legs.

"That stays in," he rumbles as he pushes it back into my pussy. I giggle, because of course that doesn't work, and eventually he gives up with a grumpy huff that is so typical of this man, and says, "I'll put more inside you."

I sit up enough to trace over his chest with my hands. He's so utterly gorgeous. He watches me with hooded, hungry eyes.

"I can't believe I can touch you." I think of all the days I yearned to see him like this. To be familiar with the big, gruff man who filled my thoughts.

"You always could."

"Really?" I check his face, and his expression is gently amused.

"All you ever had to do was ask. That was my only condition. I wasn't going to let you go, but neither was I going to take anything you didn't ask for."

"I could have asked," I say in wonder. And I, stupidly, told myself I would never request anything because I was convinced he didn't want me.

"Da." He nods again, voice sincere. "What else do you need, moya koshechka? You have all the time in the world to tell me. I'll give you anything."

"A baby," I say with a touch of fear, despite everything that's just happened. What's said during sex could just be talk, right? "I want a family."

"Already certain. I was quite serious about that." He digs his fingers into my side, possessively and my heart melts with delight. "What else?"

"I want to see you smile." It's a frivolous request, but he's the most important thing to me. I'm desperate to see him pleased.

"Easy." A slow, content smile spreads across his face like snow melting in the sunshine. I take it in greedily even as I return it.

"Oh god, I..." I shake my head, laughing, disbelief and wonder bubbling through me. "I want that smile on tap."

"It's only for you," he murmurs. "As is this." He reaches to the side of the bed where he discarded his trousers and feels around until he withdraws a solitaire diamond ring.

My mouth falls open.

"Hand," he demands softly, and I obey. As it slides over my knuckle, it's like the click of a lock. I examine it from every angle as Brody looks on indulgently.

I'm engaged to a mafia boss. I couldn't be happier.

It's many thank-you kisses and distractions later that we're lying together again, this time facing each other on our sides.

"What about the rest of the Italian mafia? There were more than two of them, right?" I ask. "Do I need to hide out here?" Not a hardship so long as Brody is with me.

"Not fully dealt with," he concedes. "I still have the head of the snake to cut off."

It's the answer I dreaded, and yet, for all his bloodthirsty ways, I trust this man. He tended my wounds. He saved me. However dangerous he is to others, he'll be the best husband and father. I don't doubt that for a second.

"Okay. I'll stay for as long as you need in this safe house," I reply lightly. "I'll be your captive."

A slow smile develops on his face again and it's getting easier for him, I think. He reaches out and rests the backs of his fingers on my face, stroking my cheek with his thumb.

"Everywhere is your safe house when you're with me."

I thought my heart couldn't expand further, but it does.

"I would die to protect you," he murmurs as he looks into my eyes, sincerity in his. "There's nothing I wouldn't do for the woman I love. Those men who hurt you were just the beginning. Anything it takes. Any sacrifice. I'd kill any number of men to keep you safe and by my side, moya koshechka."

"Brody. My angel." I pull him closer to me, his warm heat enveloping me. He's been my Dark Angel, looking over me, for three years. And now he's mine. "I love you."

18

BRODY

Three months later

The happiest moment of my life is seeing my bride step onto the lawn as the music swells. The sun is shining, and well-dressed guests including a who's who of the London Mafia Syndicate since Caterina is now in their book club and has told me I have to be nice to them, are sitting in neat rows in our walled garden.

And I'm the luckiest man in the world.

Caterina looks stunning. She takes my breath away. This girl is the sun, my everything. The source of all the good things in my life, and I'm so grateful that she somehow loves a grumpy mafia boss twice her age.

A little sob comes from the front row, but I don't look over to see who it is. I already know, and my smile widens.

"Doesn't she look beautiful?" says Caterina's mother. "My baby is all grown up."

I found Caterina's parents in the Cayman islands, as expected. It was a cute family reunion. While they weren't delighted about her choice of fiancé being a mafia boss, they didn't take too much persuading. They love her, and since she's glowing with early pregnancy and being spoiled to within an inch of her life, they gave their blessing. I think my reassurances about the Geraci mafia having been disposed of helped, too.

"She's a credit to you, Mrs Hart." But what I mean is that Caterina is a credit to herself. It's her hard work that made this wedding as stunning as it is. She chose everything, I just gave her a bank account in her name with a lot of money in it and said yes to her every idea.

She holds my gaze as she walks down the aisle between the guests. At her side is her father, but I only see her. And when she reaches me, and takes my hand, my chest is an expanding balloon that threatens to lift me off my feet from sheer happiness. I could hold Caterina to me and float away.

But thankfully, my heart only feels light. This sensation is still unfamiliar after decades of snapping and growling at everyone. Caterina marrying me is more than I deserve.

And when she repeats her vows with so much love in her eyes, and slides a thick platinum band onto my finger, I can't resist catching her hand to press an illicit kiss onto her soft palm. I enjoy every moment of our wedding ceremony, because Caterina crafted it.

After the formalities that make her officially mine, there's a reception in the garden. The same one where we finally understood each other. Caterina is busy hugging people and being perfect. All I have to do is stand by her side like a very protective and pleased gargoyle. I love watching her so happy.

"Congratulations," says a voice to me.

"Thank you." I don't look away from Caterina.

"Worked out well in the end, didn't it." The voice is posh. And not good at taking a hint.

"Yes."

"How did you get on with the Italians?"

"Fine," I reply.

Caterina laughs as her mother exclaims loudly about how proud she is of her daughter with her Business Studies degree. The university was very understanding about the alternative exam arrangements, after I made a substantial donation.

"Angel, you've married her. You can take your eyes off your wife for two minutes. I'm sure you're aware of object permanence. She won't disappear if you're not looking at her," the kingpin of Westminster drawls.

To make a point, I stroke Caterina's shoulder and kiss the top of her head in a leisurely fashion, before I murmur to her, "I love you, I just need to speak with a self-important zhopa."

She nods and clasps my hand briefly.

"I know Russian swear words," Westminster says dryly as I turn to him. "That's mild. Try harder if you want to insult me."

We regard each other. The best-known kingpin in London, and the Shadow.

"There's something you'll be interested to see," I tell him, and he nods.

We head across the lawn as Steve emerges from the house. Just the person I wanted to catch.

"Come with us," I order, but slacken my pace to account for his lingering injuries.

The older man hides his pain as we take a second flight of cream stone stairs down into the cellar.

Westminster gives a low whistle as I guide them

through the arched rooms all racked with bottles. "Nice stash."

"Thank you."

"We'll have to talk about some swaps, one day." Westminster eyes the labels as we walk past. "I have an excellent store, but it's a lot more whisky. Whereas you have some truly lovely wine."

I didn't bring them down here for that, so I don't answer. In the furthest of the first set of cellar rooms, there's a mostly-empty rack.

"Boss." Steve tries to help as I drag it out. "I can..." He trails off as I squat down, careful to not get dust on my suit.

I lift a circular wooden trapdoor and a stale smell rises.

"What the hell is this?" Steve asks, peering over the edge of the revealed hole.

"It's an oubliette," Westminster replies for me, voice hushed.

"What's that?" Steve is none the wiser.

"A deep hole," I reply.

"It's from the French, 'to forget'." Westminster folds his arms. "It's a medieval torture and death device."

"You said I had no class, and I was too impatient." I gesture at the oubliette. "Does this meet your standards?"

Not that it matters. My wife's approval is the only thing I need.

Westminster sighs, but there's a hint of a smile around his mouth. "Dark Angel indeed. This wasn't quite what I had in mind when I said last month that justice occasionally took time."

Steve flicks his gaze between Westminster and me, and trembles. "Please, Boss. I didn't mean for anything to happen to your wife. I swear I was paying attention. I won't fail you again."

"There's always room..." I pretend to ponder aloud.

"He didn't send you to the best hospitals in London, pay for physiotherapy, and have you as his best man at his wedding only to throw you down here," Westminster reassures Steve with a wry look. "If he wanted either of us dead, we'd already have a bullet in our skull."

True, though saving someone only to kill them more slowly, is not a bad idea, as torture goes. I nod in agreement. "I brought you because I thought you'd like to see the revenge on the leader whose men put you in hospital."

Steve sags a little in relief. "So..."

"The Geraci kingpin," I confirm. The mafia who went after Caterina and her family.

"How long has he been in there?" Steve asks.

One week, three days, and approximately five hours. "I forget."

"Do you think he's dead?" Now staring at the black hole with morbid fascination, Steve seems to have recovered from the fear that I was going to shove him into the oubliette.

"I don't know."

"Normally, you prefer the 'shoot first, ask questions later' tactic. I'm surprised you controlled yourself this time." Westminster can't resist a peek into the darkness either.

I don't look. There's nothing to see but black.

"My wife stood at the back of a cupboard in the dark for three hours, petrified for her life." The familiar anger flows through my blood. It's almost calming now that I've dealt with everyone involved and Caterina is mine. "The oubliette is shaped like a bottle. He can lie down."

"Generous of you," Westminster says, with a touch of sarcasm.

"How deep is it?" Steve asks, turning his head to examine the stone walls that are akin to a well.

"Twelve feet to the bottom, though it seems it would have been deeper originally. The floor presumably was built up a little over the centuries with whatever was thrown in."

Steve blanches and steps away from the entrance.

"Mmm. You don't want to fall down there," I say. "Probably would break several bones."

A low sound like a dying animal reverberates up.

We all hear it.

My hands curl into fists and I wish I'd just killed the zasranets man immediately.

"We'll return to the party now." I've spent too long away from my wife already. "But another time, I can get the drone out so you can look if you're curious—"

"This is not how the London Mafia Syndicate approves of dealing with conflicts," Westminster interrupts me.

"Mmm." It's nothing more than an acknowledgement.

There's a hush full of the awareness that I didn't have to show Westminster this, and could have killed the man in the oubliette immediately. I don't want to pull that bastard out, but he isn't yet dead. That's all the concession Westminster gets.

And he seems to know that. "I appreciate your change in practice."

"For this mafia leader. The others..." I take out my phone and ping him the file I have with the names, list of notable activities, and photographs of the men I killed in my quest for vengeance against all who hurt Caterina. The two who directly hurt her, and those stupid enough to be found hurting women or children when my need to kill was on a hair trigger.

Westminster pulls out his phone and scans the document. His eyebrows raise. "Geraci was involved with..."

"Yes," I confirm. Neither of us speak further, but we share a glance of mutual disgust.

Westminster pockets his phone. "Understood."

A croak echoes up from the hole. Weaker this time.

Rage flares again in my chest, but Westminster's expression is impassive.

"How long did you say he's been in there?" In contrast, the lines of Steve's face crease with concern.

"He's probably dead by now," Westminster lies calmly. "And we have a marriage to celebrate, and a family reunited."

"Exactly." And a family begun. Pride flows through me remembering again that my wife is pregnant under that pure white dress.

Steve straightens, as though coming from a trance. "How about we just forget about this whole thing?"

I close the trapdoor and the three of us move the racking back into place. Then the cellar is dead silent again.

"Now." I turn a couple of bottles on the rack, pretending to search. "This space is almost empty, but I have some excellent wine arriving next week that will be stored here for twenty or more years."

I pull out champagne and pass it to Steve and Westminster. "I think you'll enjoy these. They're properly aged and chilled."

"Served cold, you might say, Boss." Steve accepts two bottles.

Westminster lets out a bark of laughter. "But isn't revenge supposed to be sweet, not sparkling?"

"Revenge is ice cream. Sweet and served cold." Maybe

Caterina's humour is rubbing off on me. "But we'll have to make do with champagne."

We chuckle as we climb the stairs out of the cellar, and at the door, I switch off the lights.

Back in the garden, Steve and Westminster take charge of the alcohol we just acquired, and I search the crowd until I find the most beautiful woman in the world, wearing a white dress. She's with her mother and a group of the London Mafia Syndicate women, sunlight spilling all over them, making them shine.

They part as I approach, and I take Caterina's hand and interlock our fingers as she's mid-sentence.

"She'll be back in a minute. I just need a moment with my bride."

There's a chorus of "ahhh" and "so cute" as I draw Caterina away. I intend to only go far enough to speak alone and kiss her in privacy, but my feet take us to the entrance of the maze.

"Angel," she murmurs, leaning into me and squeezing my hand as she sees it.

But I only pull her out of sight and drag her against me as I sink my back into the firm outer hedge, surrounding us with the scent of the leaves as I claim her mouth in a kiss. It's several minutes before I ease off consuming her.

"Much as I'd like to fuck you right here and now, looking so gorgeous, I'll wait until later when I can chase you, hold you down, and properly hear you scream your pleasure into the darkness," I promise against her lips. And this is her wedding day. I'm not risking messing up the dress and makeup she so carefully did when tonight I can rip the white lace negligee I saw her slipping into the wardrobe yesterday.

She makes a breathy little whimper and I smile as I kiss her again.

"Thank you. For everything," she says, holding the back of my neck as she stands on tiptoe to kiss me more.

"Are you having a good day?" I check.

"The best," she says against my lips. "And you?"

"It's perfect when I'm at your side." Carefully, I hold her jaw and stroke her cheek lovingly as I look into her deep brown eyes. My wife. I'll never let her go. I'll never let anything bad happen to her again. "A day to remember."

EPILOGUE
CATERINA

10 YEARS LATER

People who say you can have too much of a good thing have clearly never met my husband.

I peek around the door to the twins' room to watch Brody read them a bedtime story.

It's their birthday tomorrow, and when I shooed them upstairs to bathe after their two younger siblings had already been washed, they were hyped up with excitement. But they're both now calm and entranced by their dad reading to them.

He does excellent voices. I've tried to tell him he should do audiobooks. His are the best growly man dragons, and sweetest girl dragons. I bet he'd do rough and sexy romance heroes who would cause mass swooning events, even as mothers everywhere insisted they only followed his social media because their children adored his kids' book's characters.

He's making this dragon book so good I'm honestly listening, despite having read it to the twins at least a hundred times.

"And then, the red dragon roared out red flames. Raaaahhhhh!"

I grin. He gets so into reading to the children, my sulky, grumpy quiet husband. He's still a scary shadow of a mafia boss. My Dark Angel remains part rumour, part legend, part hushed disbelief when some lowlife goes missing.

But the Dark Angel will laugh with his babies. He's bright and fun with them.

And with me.

I keep watching as he reads, the soft glow highlighting the planes of his face. He has more silver hairs now, but I love that even more. He says he loves my stretch marks in the same way, and certainly he has shown no signs of enjoying my body any less.

Quite the opposite, in fact.

I can't believe I get to see him whenever I want. The years of longing—we laugh sometimes when remembering our mutual pining—are a distant memory. Almost forgotten. The story of how we met has taken on a rosy hue with time, and us being together with our kids is the source of so much joy it's hard to remember it wasn't always like this.

He's been a doting father from the beginning, and loves nothing more than when I'm pregnant, or when he has a baby to carry when we walk in the garden. The children are strictly forbidden from the maze, and we say it's because they might get lost. But it's at least as much because we don't want them seeing us doing some more baby-making, imaginary or not.

"Then, the blue dragon roared out blue flames. Blllaaaahhhhh!" Brody says, changing voice seamlessly.

I giggle and Brody sees me from the corner of his eye. He gives no visible sign of his split attention as he continues to read, but there's a smirk that tugs at his mouth.

The kids are almost asleep, watching him with hooded eyes and teddy bears clutched to them.

"Then, the violet dragon roared out violet flames. Vaaaaahhhhh!"

Nine years old tomorrow, our first babies are tucked up in bed. Our other two are six and three, and we have yet to decide on whether we'll have one more.

"And that is how a rainbow is made." Brody closes the book with a snap.

"Again," comes sleepily from one of the kids.

As Brody chuckles softly, and kisses both the twins good night, I think we will have another child. Just to hold on to this sweetness of my husband reading for them a little longer.

He turns off the lamps, checks the nightlight, then herds me out of the bedroom and closes the door behind him with an almost silent click and gathers me into his arms.

"You know," he says conversationally, "in the Greek tradition, children's birthdays are a celebration for the mother."

"Really?" I say, distracted by his closeness. I breathe in the delicious neroli, steel, musk, and sea water scent of him.

"Apparently so. A new Greek mafia acquaintance was telling me. Mothers do all the work, no?"

I snort. I do plenty, yes. But Brody makes it sound like he's nothing more than the sperm donor, when yesterday he was on his knees playing with the kids.

"If you say so."

"I have a special present for you, moya koshechka." My husband blinks at me, smiling his subtle, smug smile that means he has something truly devious planned. "Come to bed and find out what it is."

EXTENDED EPILOGUE
BRODY

10 YEARS LATER, LATER THAT NIGHT

Caterina is a little mistrustful as I tie her to our bed. She's naked after her evening shower, and while we've had many years to explore all the pleasures of each other, she knows I love to try new things with her.

"It's okay," I reassure her as her breathing goes ragged when she sees the blindfold I bring out.

"What are you planning?"

"Good girls find out when they accept their blindfolds."

She sighs and smiles as she closes her eyes and accepts the soft black cloth over her eyes.

I undress and my cock is inevitably hard from binding her hands and feet, spread before me.

"So beautiful, and all mine," I murmur as I trail a finger over her nipples. I've kissed every inch of my wife. I do so regularly.

"Yes, all yours." She nods in agreement and I love that.

I take the opportunity to kneel between her thighs and

stroke over her soft thighs and admire her slick pink folds. "You have a gorgeous cunt."

She whimpers.

My mouth waters as I lean down and kiss over her thighs. I adore the taste of this sweet girl, but I like teasing her even more. I linger over the secret places of her body. The curve of her arse, the seam where her leg meets her torso. All the while, she squirms, desperate for more.

Eventually, I reach that perfect little slit. She quivers as I lick over her folds, then press my lips to her clit. I kiss and nibble, but more than anything I tease and drag my tongue over her again and again, until she's dripping, and moaning.

And then, I draw back.

"Brody!" she complains as soon as I do, and I laugh. The joy of playing with Caterina is so strong it's almost tangible.

"That was an evil laugh," she grumbles, and arches her back, offering up her pussy to me. She knows she's tempting me. "Please. Please, husband."

"Mmm, I do love it when you beg," I croon, and tweak her nipple.

Her gasp of surprise at the sudden pleasure-pain broadens my smile into a full grin and I rise, drawing the toy box from underneath the bed. It takes me a second to pull out the new vibrator I bought for her.

"What are you doing?" she asks, voice breathy but alert.

"Moya koshechka," I reply patiently. "If I didn't want it to be a surprise, don't you think I'd let you see?"

Her mouth curves into a smirk. "Will I like it?"

"Would I have you spread on the bed, your lovely cunt exposed for me, and unable to move, if I thought you'd accept without a fight?" It's a tease though. For one, if she fights it's only to enhance both our pleasure, and for the thrill of having me hold her down. And two, she'll do anything I ask. My wife trusts me, and knows I'd pull out all my teeth without anaesthetic before I hurt her.

But drawing out her sexual pleasure to the point it's agony? That's fair.

I take the vibrator—it's shaped like a compact "n"—and nudge the insertable tip at Caterina's needy hole, and she squeaks and writhes.

"Is that you?" She tosses her head, sensing something is different from when I fuck her like this. Which I do, and we both like.

"In a way?" I push it further into her and I stroke her thigh comfortingly. Her wet, slick passage sucks in the toy. "A needy little cunt you have, moya koshechka."

"Mmm." She rolls her hips experimentally, then her mouth twists with dissatisfaction. "That's... It? It's not as big as your cock."

I chuckle. "It's not."

The evidence is right in front of me, bobbing up above my belly button. I glide my hand down my length, then pump the head a few times, arousal coiling at the base of my spine as I take Caterina in. She's so utterly mine, in moments like this. Unable to do anything but take what I give her.

The impulse to yank out the toy and fuck her hard skitters over my skin, but I resist. Plenty of time to do that later. And while it hasn't lost its novelty—sex with Caterina never will—I am interested in more perverted pleasures than simply having my cock in her wet pussy tonight.

And standing over Caterina's helpless, naked body, her exposed for my whim, is so delightfully filthy. She's still much younger than me, her body a bit curvier after four children, but nonetheless gorgeous. Caterina remains the one who turns me on like no other.

I can't see as much as I'd like, with the toy inserted and covering her clit. I adjust it so the clitoral suction part entirely fits over her clit.

Then, one hand on my cock, I pull out the remote control and turn on the toy to its lowest setting. This vibrator was the best rated and most expensive one in the tasteful online store. Caterina tilts her head thoughtfully and shifts, getting used to the sensation. It's got all sorts of settings, but I just put on the basic, all over thing and fist my cock, admiring my wife's phenomenal body.

"I think I was ."

I press the button to increase the vibrations a few times.

"I hope it wasn't... ohhh."

The laughter bubbles from me as Caterina's mouth falls open and she pants.

"Mmm, you were saying?" I tease, notching up the intensity with one more click. That's hitting the spot, clearly. I like this new vibrator.

"Brody!" It's half a moan and half a plea. Her chest has gone pink, and she's beginning to shake.

"You're so perfect. Enjoy it," I tell her as I stroke my cock more vigorously. I eat her up with my eyes.

There's a luxury in using a toy because I get to fully enjoy seeing her whole body wracked with pleasure. I can take in the curl of her toes, the way her soft belly rises and falls, the little movements of her hips, and the way her head stretches back. I can even peek around the toy and see how her pussy is throbbing. Arousal is leaking out of her hole.

"Do you like that, moya koshechka?"

She makes a wordless sound of need, her legs trembling.

"I think you do. Such a good girl, taking that toy as I stroke my cock and watch you."

This time it's a high-pitched sob.

"I'm going to come all over you," I inform her. "You're a filthy, lovely, hot little pussy and when you've come for me, I'll cover your greedy slit and that soft belly with my come."

She nods and whines.

"Such a come-slut," I tease. "You want it don't you? Give in, and come for me, and I'll paint you with my seed." I click the setting one higher and she bucks, her pretty face creasing with pleasure as it tips her over. She thrashes on the bed and it's a good thing she's tied down. She cries out my name and arches her back as she comes.

I groan, and only just manage to change the setting to afterglow so it's not too much for her, because my hand is pumping on my cock and I can't take my eyes off my girl overcome with pleasure. I shift so I'm kneeling over her and fist my cock tight, hammering over the sensitive tip as I watch her.

The pulses and jerks she makes as her orgasm sweeps over her tip me over, and I come with a shout. The ecstasy shudders down my limbs, pushing outwards from my cock, seemingly in every direction—outwards, spurting onto Caterina's naked tits, and through my torso and down my legs in tingling, electrifying pulses.

I come, spilling over her belly and right up to her tits. It even goes a bit further than I expect, and hits her throat. It's a primal claim, as savage as ownership and collars and the rings on both of our fingers. She's mine, and I love showing her that as much as I have to have the civilised, outward signs.

It's a white starburst of pleasure that flares out over and over, pushing out more and more come, covering her with my seed. I'm light-headed with how good it feels, kneeling over my tied up captive wife.

"My god," Caterina breathes a few minutes later, after the last of my orgasm has receded.

I need to see her eyes.

I fall forward, bracing myself over her.

"My love," I murmur as I undo her blindfold. She blinks up at me. "How was that?"

Her smile is a bit saucy. "That was... Not quite as good as your cock inside me from behind and your fingers on my clit, but totally acceptable."

"Good, happy birth-day to you, mother of my children. Congratulations. You did exceptionally well birthing and raising them."

She grins back. "Thank you. Your considerable contributions are very much appreciated too."

"These ones?" I ask, smearing my come over her breasts.

"Especially those," she agrees as I caress her, stroking the liquid all over her.

"You're such a mess." I wipe my hand on her thigh, and she giggles.

"Look who made me a dirty girl."

"You're my good girl."

She purrs with contentment at being told that and I methodically undo her restraints. Seconds later, she's sitting up, has grabbed the back of my head and is kissing me, careless of the come dripping down her chest.

I growl and pull her into my arms. "Dirty girls need to get clean."

In our en suite, I wash Caterina in the massive walk-in hot shower, taking particular care of her breasts and ordering her to open her legs for me so I can kneel at her feet and wash her there too. Although, strictly, I'm not in the least dirty, Caterina insists on running her hands over every part of me, too. And after far too long in the shower, that has the inevitable result. I'm hard once more.

She makes me as horny as a teenager.

When we're definitely clean, and both wrapped in fluffy white towels, Caterina presses herself to me. Her little hand finds its way between the towel and between my legs and she murmurs her happiness as she smooths up and down my length.

It's late now, and the kids will be awake early.

"Again?" I suggest. Who cares if tomorrow we're tired? We'll cope. I need to make love to Caterina.

"Please," she whispers back.

"Anything for my wife." I discard our towels, lift her into my arms, and carry her back to our bed. Laying her down, I cover her body with mine, and kiss her lips and confess, yet again, "I love you."

She writhes beneath me, kissing me back and tangling her hands in my hair. It's so intimate, so close. Sexy and loving in a different way to how we made love earlier. The delight of skin on skin is everlasting with Caterina. And she's right, however good kinky games are, this is the love we can't do without.

"I love you too," she whispers as she wraps her legs around my waist and wriggles until the head of my erection is right at her entrance. "And I need you."

"I'm yours," I promise as I push into her. Every time it's like the first time. "And you're *mine*."

THANKS

Thank you for reading, I hope you enjoyed it.

Want to read a little more Happily Ever After? Click to get exclusive epilogues and free stories! or head to EvieRoseAuthor.com

If you have a moment, I'd really appreciate a review wherever you like to talk about books. Reviews, however brief, help readers find stories they'll love.

Love to get the news first? Follow me on your favored social media platform - I love to chat to readers and you get all the latest gossip.

If the newsletter is too much like commitment, I recommend following me on BookBub, where you'll just get new release notifications and deals.

- amazon.com/author/evierose
- bookbub.com/authors/evie-rose
- instagram.com/evieroseauthor
- tiktok.com/@EvieRoseAuthor

INSTALOVE BY EVIE ROSE

Stalker Kingpins

Spoiled by my Stalker

From the moment we lock eyes, I'm his lucky girl... But there's a price to pay

Owned by her Enemy

I didn't expect the ruthless new kingpin—an older man, gorgeous and hard—to extract such a price for a ceasefire: an arranged marriage.

His Public Claim

My first time is sold to my brother's best friend

Pregnant by the Mafia Boss

Kingpin's Baby

I beg the Kingpin for help... And he offers marriage.

Baby Proposal

My boss walked in on me buying "magic juice" online... And now he's demanding to be my baby's daddy!

Grumpy Bosses

Older Hotter Grumpier

My billionaire boss catches me reading when I should be working. And the punishment...?

Tall, Dark, and Grumpy

When my boss comes to fetch me from a bar, I'm expecting him to go nuts that I'm drunk and described my fake boyfriend just like him. But he demands marriage...

London Mafia Bosses

Captured by the Mafia Boss

I might be an innocent runaway, but I'm at my friend's funeral to avenge her murder by the mafia boss: King.

Taken by the Kingpin

Tall, dark, older and dangerous, I shouldn't want him.

Stolen by the Mafia King

I didn't know he has been watching me all this time.

I had a plan to escape. Everything is going perfectly at my wedding rehearsal dinner until *he* turns up.

Caught by the Kingpin

The kingpin growls a warning that I shouldn't try his patience by attempting to escape.

There's no way I'm staying as his little prisoner.

Claimed by the Mobster

I'm in love with my ex-boyfriend's dad: a dangerous and powerful mafia boss twice my age.

Snatched by the Bratva

I have an excruciating crush on this man who comes into the coffee shop. Every day. He's older, gorgeous, perfectly dressed. He has a Russian accent and silver eyes.

Kidnapped by the Mafia Boss

I locked myself in the bathroom when my date pulled out a knife. Then a tall dark rescuer crashed through the door... and kidnapped me.

Held by the Bratva

"Who hurt you?"

Before I know it, my gorgeous neighbour has scooped me up into his arms and taken me to his penthouse. And he won't let me go.

Seized by the Mafia King

I'm kidnapped from my wedding

Filthy Scottish Kingpins

Forbidden Appeal

He's older and rich, and my teenage crush re-surfaces as I beg the former kingpin to help me escape a mafia arranged marriage. He stares at me like I'm a temptress he wants to banish, but we're snowed in at his Scottish castle.

Captive Desires

I was sent to kill him, but he's captured me, and I'm at his mercy. He says he'll let me go if I beg him to take his...

Eager Housewife

Her best friend's dad is advertising for a free use convenient housewife, and she's the perfect applicant.

Printed in Dunstable, United Kingdom